POISONED IVY

A DARK ROMANCE NOVEL

D.W. MARSHALL

ISBN: 978-0-9968729-3-5

Library of Congress Control Number: 2016946382

Cover design by D.W. Marshall

Edited by AuthorsAssistant.com

Printed in the United States

To Phil, I miss you every single day.

CELTIC AND IRISH NAME PRONUNCIATION GUIDE

Maeve (May-vee)
Ailbhe (Al-vee)
Lugh (Loo)
Saoirse (Sear-sha)
Ciara (Kee-ra)

1

MAEVE: COUNTING THE DAYS

*I*t has been nine months since I was nabbed from the athletic club and brought to The Chamber. That is: two hundred and seventy days; six thousand four hundred and eighty hours; three hundred eighty-eight thousand, eight hundred minutes; and twenty-three million, three hundred and twenty-eight thousand seconds. Yes, I am counting, because each and every passing, precious second, minute, hour, and day means that even though I have lost a little more of myself, I am closer to going home. Closer to shedding the name Ivy and all of the horror that comes with it. That is, if Mason stays true to his word our first night here, and we are actually released. I'm not sure that there will be enough of me to make it home. But whatever is left, I will drag it home and my love will help me become whole again.

You see, I am not as strong as the other girls. I have always had what my mother called "a fragile constitution" growing up, probably because I am not a stranger to traumatic events.

Mason has amassed quite the spread. Most of the girls here are strong, and will most likely leave this tragic experience even stronger, with battle wounds that they will wear as badges. I believe that those are the type of girls that the sadistic Mason Wilde should shoot for, because his aim was off on a few of us.

Me, Violet, and Sunshine are the weakest links in the chain, and we may not survive.

Raven is my roommate and I have seen her in action. She is calculating, always watching, always studying. She hasn't shed one visible tear since the day we got here. She may look like a beauty queen, but she is tough as nails. Sapphire, I swear, is enjoying herself here. I wouldn't be surprised if she asked to stay on and work here at the end of our year.

If there is an end.

Sky, who I believe belongs in our group of weaklings, is so damn positive I'd think she was on drugs, if I thought she could get them here. So just because of her cheery attitude, I place her among the strong. Then there is Flame. She has her very own knight in shining armor for a guard. Not that she needs one—she is unbreakable. I am shocked that the rest of us have made it this far.

I pull out my pad and paper and begin to scribe another letter to Keegan. We would be nearing a year of marriage if I hadn't been taken.

My Dearest Keegan,

I can't imagine what you must be going through not knowing what happened to me. Nine months is a long time. I can only hope that you are still waiting for me, that you believe I will come back to you. This place is hell. I hope our love is strong enough to survive the things that I have suffered here, because the only way I will overcome this is knowing that I have you.

You know, in the beginning, I used to pretend I was with you every time I was with one of them. It worked for a while, but I think my brain caught on and won't let me lie to myself anymore. Each day I am breaking into pieces.

Three more months. I need to survive three more months. I will see you soon. I believe that. I love you so much and can't wait to become your wife.

Yours forever,
Maeve

I DON'T KNOW if I will ever show these letters to Keegan. Mostly, I write them for myself. They allow me to speak aloud what is on my mind. Keegan really is the very best part of me. We met when his family moved to Dublin. I was eighteen, Keegan was twenty. We hit it off well because we both shared an American and Irish connection. Keegan was born in Dublin, a Flanagan, but grew up in the States. His father is Irish, his mother a famous American actress who met his father while filming a movie in Ireland. I was born to Irish parents, an O'Malley, and I have the red hair and freckles to prove it. I am a ginger through and through. But I am not Irish born. I have citizenship in both countries, but I was born in America, and my family moved back to Ireland when I was in fifth grade. Keegan and I became fast friends, sharing some of our favorite American and Irish customs.

Before I turned nineteen we were a couple. It was only natural that I wanted to marry him. He was what my mother and I called "dashing." Worldly, ambitious, romantic, and adventurous. He was the kind of guy who made you feel alive whenever you were in his presence. I can't remember a moment where he was unkind. In a word, he was perfect. Now, in a few months I will be returning to him —hopefully—and I pray that I am still enough.

2

MAEVE: HOME

I miss the streets of Dalkey, a quaint suburb of Dublin and our little slice of coastal heaven. I realize now how deprived I have been of my sight. For a year we were only allowed to gaze among the walls of The Chamber, unless you count the pool party we had while there, when Mason opened up the skylight and allowed us to feel an actual breeze and catch a view of the cloudy sky above. I don't count that. That was only enough to make us crave what we wanted that much more.

Now I am cruising through the streets of my favorite city, in the back of a sedan, on my way home. I never thought this day would arrive.

Freedom.

Rich and free.

Not that money was ever an issue for me. My family is part of a royal line. On my twenty-fifth birthday I will inherit a fortune, so Mason's four-million-dollar payoff may not mean as much to me as the other girls. But I took it anyway. He owes us millions and more for our year of sex slavery. I wish there was a way to use the money to help me forget. Or we could pool our money together to find him and put him in a cell where he belongs. I know that I am not strong enough for that mission, so I must focus on deleting this trauma from my mind, like I did the first time. Then again, I was just a girl the first time, and my brain had a lot more time to stow away the things that happened to me. But the answer to my path to healing is only a short distance away. Keegan. He can fix me. His love will give me the strength to power through this.

The breeze upon my face is everything to me right now. I don't think I will take another simple pleasure for granted again. When we pull up to my house my stomach is in knots as the nerves creep up on me. Dreaming of returning home and actually being here are two different things. I have wanted to walk up to this house and through my front door more than life, but now that I am here all I want to do is vomit on the floor of this nice sedan. The questions, the uncertainty of returning to my life are all weighing down on me.

I sit in the backseat and stare out at my home. It is nothing compared to the lavish Chamber, but it is beautiful to me. Lush grass that seems to go on forever, with a miniature castle-like structure smack dab in the middle. That is home for me—seven bedrooms, a small theater, ten bathrooms. I'm not rich at all, but Ma and Da are. Their status is one of the reasons we moved back to Ireland, because of what happened to me when we were in the United States. My Da felt he could protect me better in his homeland, but I guess he was wrong.

"Home," I whisper. It is as beautiful as I remember, a painting come to life. Filled with people who love me and have no doubt missed me. My Ma and Da, and twin little brothers, Ailbhe and Lugh.

The driver starts down the long, tree-lined driveway. I shake my nerves and worries. This is my home.

"You can let me out here. I want to walk," I tell him. He starts to get out of the car, but before he can, I throw the door open and take off into the lush grass toward home. Giggles bounce off me as I run full speed toward my family, the home I love so much, and to Keegan. It's April in Dublin. The flowers are in bloom; the trees are bulging with life. I never thought I could miss something as simple as a tree, but I did. If anyone catches me, I will look insane for sure, but I can't resist as I wrap my arms around a healthy, full-grown oak. Of course my arms can't begin to contain its girth. "Hi, Mr. Oak Tree, I'm home!"

I release the oak and proceed to greet and smell the divine purple, pink and red blossoms and bushes. Coming home feels like being reborn. Every scent stronger, every sight brighter.

When I get to the front entry I feel the butterflies. Still, I proceed because there is only love inside. I ring the bell over and over. No one is home. The wind whooshes out of my sails a bit, because I sorta expected a huge and emotional homecoming. Instead I have to walk around the side of the house to find the spare key. It is hidden underneath a plant inside a ceramic elephant, but it's not the cliché hiding place—for ours you have to enter a six-digit code on the side of the elephant, and push down on the garden elephant's trunk in order to access it. Thankfully, the key is there.

I unlock the door and run the spare key back to its hiding spot out of habit. Ma would say, "If you never put the key back, it won't be there when you need it." I miss my ma so much. The smells that are assaulting me are so familiar. This time of year the outside of our home is a floral bouquet for the senses.

Opening the front door is like opening a present on Christmas morning or your birthday, I take a few deep breaths and push the door open. The warm scents of home hit me: my mother's bog-standard candles of warm spices and baked apples. *Mmm.*

If you asked me a year ago if I thought I would ever be here again, see my family again, I would have said that I highly doubted it.

How do you trust a monster?

I guess I—we—should be thankful that we were in the hands of *this* monster. He might have been evil and cruel for taking us away from all that we were, but he never lied to us. We were treated very well, and our release date came like he said it would. Doesn't mean that I don't hate him with every inch of my being, but for my release I thank him.

My home is a mixture of things Irish, from our farmhouse table, Ma's candles, the beautiful tapestries, and my favorite brick stove, to my favorite American things, like our sectional sofa and our monster-sized flat screen television.

It is so strange to feel as if I never left home. Everything is the same. Our kitchen, like most, is the hub for the family. When I enter my family kitchen, I feel the spirit of everyone I love so very much. "Tea. I need tea." If there was one thing that I missed this year it was a good cup of Irish tea. I find the cast iron teapot in its usual spot, fill it with water and wait. "A watched pot never boils," is what my ma always says, but for some reason my attention is on the pot, and the pot alone. Tears well up in my eyes and suddenly this teapot is the single most important thing in the world to me, because it means I am home.

"As I live and breathe." My ma's heavy brogue fills the room.

I dare look up. I know I will fall apart when I see her.

There she is. People say that I am her mini-me, and I never agreed with them until now. Her skin is milky, with a healthy share of freckles like mine. She is lithe, with bright blue-green eyes that are misting as she gazes into mine. In the seconds that follow, each one of my brothers and my da crash into the back of Ma, since she stopped at once.

"Criminy, Melanie, why did you stop like that? I spilled my coffee all over me," my da complains from the end of the line.

"Da, it's Maeve!" Ailbhe shouts, and pushes past Ma, running toward me. Lugh follows close behind. My brothers are the most adorable seven-year-old twins. Identical, with dark hair and blue eyes like our da's. They crash into me.

I squeeze the life out of my baby brothers. How can anyone be so cruel and separate a family like this? I send out a silent prayer to my Chamber sisters for their happy return home. The strong ones who I know will come out on top and the weak ones, like me, who may not survive at all. Then I squeeze the boys even tighter.

It is a dream. For the second time in my life I am reunited with my family. The first time, my brothers weren't born yet. My ma still hasn't moved from the spot where she stopped. Her hand covers her mouth and her eyes continue to rain tears.

The next pair of eyes I see belong to Da. He gazes at me, and lets out a deep breath, one he has most likely been holding onto for the entire time that I have been gone.

"My dear, sweet Maeve." He runs to me and wraps his arms around me and the boys who will probably never let me go.

I look to where my ma was standing and she is gone. "Where did Ma go?"

My da glances back to where Ma was standing. "Follow me. I will show you," he says. His voice is musical and sounds like home.

We walk out of the kitchen and into the sitting room. It is difficult to take steps because the boys won't let me go, and Da has ahold of one of my hands. My ma is kneeling in front of a candle, praying. We stand and watch, before my da guides us to join her. As a family we give thanks for my safe return. When my ma is finished she crawls over to me on her knees and wraps me into an embrace and weeps.

"My dear, sweet daughter, how I prayed for you to come back to us, and you are here. I might have just died and gone to heaven." She wipes her eyes and then my eyes. "Peter, is our darling daughter really here?"

"Yes, love."

Then we all wrap our arms around each other.

My ma, being a strong woman, gathers herself together. "I saw you were brewing up a pot of good Irish tea. I know it's your favorite, my love. Let me dish that up for you."

I follow my da toward the sofas. The boys take a seat on each side of me, so close it would be hard to tell where I begin and they end. My ma comes back with a tray full of tea for the grown-ups and milk for the boys, who still seem to not have acquired a taste for our strong Irish tea.

"What happened to you, Maeve?" My da asks the dreaded question.

I hope I will be allowed to forget this soon, but I am sure everyone in my life will want a recount of the events that happened to me. At least the parts I can repeat.

I clear my throat. "I was exercising at the fitness center like always on my days off modeling jobs. I didn't notice anything out of the ordinary when I walked out to my car. I looked around like you taught me, Da. I even had my pepper spray out. The problem is my capturers were already in my car. I managed to spray one of them in the eyes, but I didn't know there was more than one. Major drawback to having really dark windows." A tear catches in my throat. "I think that the boys should run along for the rest of this story."

Ma's face grimaces when she realizes what that might mean. "Boys, run along. We will send for you in a bit," Ma says.

"But..." They try to stay with me. But my da gives them the look he is famous for and they scoot off.

"The person in the backseat put a cloth to my face and the next thing I know I am on an airplane. This entire time I have been locked away with six other girls. Today is the first day I have been outside."

My da jumps up and sits on my right side. My ma does the same, sitting on my left side.

"I was used for sex." The words choke me on the way out. I break down.

My folks are no strangers to consoling me. They both hold me while we all cry together. "I'm calling the Garda," Da says.

I nod. I knew that was next. I was missing for a year.

OFFICER FITZGERALD and McKinley arrive within fifteen minutes of our call. I recount my story. Fitzgerald is short and stout and McKinley is tall and rail thin. They look like a caricature drawing come to life. They take notes from my story, and close their pads. Grim looks cross both of their faces.

Fitzgerald speaks up. "You haven't given us much to go on. You've no idea where you were, you were unconscious for most of the flight, and hooded when you were off the airplane, and inside some fortress until today." He shakes his head. "We will do our best, starting with the airport. You had to be on a private plane, so there should be a record," he continues.

Please do your worst. The last thing I need is a visit from the monster.
We thank them and they leave.

"I need to go to bed. I am exhausted," I say.

My parents follow me to my room, and tuck me in. They each plant a kiss on my cheek. "We love you. You rest now, dear."

I am out almost the second they leave my room.

3

MAEVE: RELIVING NIGHTMARES

ive of the seven bookcases slide open, revealing darkened staircases. The five of us who aren't virgins are instructed to take the stairs. I am trembling so hard I might break my bones. Each step I take is a death march. The man downstairs who calls himself Mason makes this place seem like an amusement park, but I promise none of us are amused. There is a draft in the stone stairwell causing me to shiver more. My teeth begin to bang into each other without my control. When I hit the top of the stairs I see that there is a room. Everything is emerald green, accented with gold. A huge bed sits in the middle of the room. I don't need anyone to spell out what that means for me. I realize that I am not alone when I hear someone clear their throat. I spin around and find a young woman standing near what looks like the entrance of a bathroom.

"I am sorry to startle you, miss. I am Iris, and I will be your groomer during your stay here."

Iris is pretty. Tall and thin, with dark brown hair and dark eyes. She has a kind face. "What is that? A groomer?" *I ask.*

She walks deeper into the green room. "I am here to make your stay bearable. I will keep you groomed and Chamber ready. After you meet your guard, I will take you on a personal tour."

As if on cue, a man walks into the room. He is very attractive as well. I am noticing a theme here. "I am Ridley." He extends his hand and I take it. Even in shock I do what is customarily polite. "I am here to keep you safe. Unless, of course, you fall asleep in your Chamber. Then I am here to fuck your brains out." I snatch my hand out of his. He offers me a menacing smile. "My post is downstairs at the base of your Chamber. There are cameras throughout your room and it is miked. If anything goes down, I will be up here in a flash."

I throw up in my mouth a little.

Can you hold your breath long enough to die? I plan to give that a try. Ridley excuses himself and disappears into the staircase.

"Okay, for the tour. This, of course, is your Chamber. Over here..." Iris walks me to a golden armoire. "Is your pleasure cabinet..."

She opens it, and I cringe. It is filled with dildos, whips, beads—things I have never seen in person. She scoops up a huge dildo and walks across the room. I don't follow her with my body. Only my eyes travel with her. I'm not sure I will be able to remain standing if I move.

"This..." She is standing next to a horse that looks as if it belongs on a carousel. She screws the dildo onto the horse's back. "Is your pleasure pony. You will most likely spend a great deal of time pleasuring yourself for the gentlemen during your stay here."

I hit the ground.

When I wake up there are five men in my emerald room. One of the men picks me up and sets me onto the pleasure pony. "Work, girl," he says.

I can't see his face. I can't see any of their faces, only their erect cocks, all waiting for their turn with me. I sink down onto the pleasure pony. Over and over I plunge the large dildo deep into myself. Tears storm from my eyes. Another faceless cock pulls me from the pony and tosses me onto the bed and all of the cocks converge on me. What started out as five keeps multiplying until the room is full of them, in my mouth, in my ass, my pussy, full of cocks.

I shoot up in bed, my own screams waking me. My door flies open and my ma and da are at my side at once. I can't catch my breath. The sobs are coming out of me in force. My parents don't say a word.

What is there to say? They wrap me in love and protection. I can hear the tears they each fight catching in their throats. Their daughter may just be the most unlucky young woman alive. My ma and da get comfortable on each side of me and that is how we fall asleep. With the protection of them, I am able to sleep without any nightmares.

4

MAEVE: ADDED PROTECTION

*W*hen I make it to the kitchen the next morning I am flooded with warmth and familiarity. The boys run and wrap me in a big hug.

"Maeve's awake, Da!" Ailbhe shouts.

"I see that, Lugh," my da says, looking over the morning paper.

"Lugh didn't say it, Da, I did." Ailbhe corrects my da.

My da just shakes his head and smiles. It is hard for us to keep up with which twin said or did what. Even their voices are identical.

I make it to the table with the boys still connected to me. "You boys take a seat and let your sister be," Ma says, shooing them with her hands.

"We can't, Ma. We missed her too much," Lugh says.

"We wanted to sleep in her room, but when we went to sneak in you and Da were in there already," Ailbhe says.

"Well I guess we all missed her, then," Ma says.

We sit as a family and enjoy a breakfast of rashers, bangers, black pudding, white pudding, eggs, tomatoes, mushrooms, potatoes, Irish beans, and soda bread. I missed my comfort foods of home more than I even knew.

The doorbell chimes. And my da gets up from his seat. "Right on time," he says and heads out of the kitchen. He returns moments later with two men dressed in suits. They are huge men, like over six feet tall and American-football-player big. "I would like you to meet Pierce O'Connor and Miles Standish," Da says, pointing to each of the men.

Pierce looks more like he could be my brother than the twins, with red hair and freckles to match mine, and skin even paler. Maybe my uncle. I can't place his age but if I had to guess I'd says early thirties. Miles is of African descent. Closer to my age, very attractive, with dark skin and hair cut close.

"Nice to meet you both," Ma says. "This is our Maeve." She points in my direction. "And these are the twins, Lugh and Ailbhe."

The three of us say hi to the men. My ma shoves a cup of Irish tea in their hands without even asking them if they want tea. She has that way about her and they must sense it because they take it without question. My da leads them into the parlor. We don't follow. It is not unusual in his line of work for him to meet with people who we aren't acquainted with.

"Did you see them, Maeve? Your new bodyguards are ginormous!" Lugh shouts out in excitement.

"My new what?" I ask, looking to Ma for answers.

She is busying herself at the kitchen sink, and doesn't respond to my question. "What have I told you and your brother about poking in on people when they are speaking, and worse, running away at the mouth about it when you shouldn't!" She scolds both of them without turning around, even though only one of them said something.

"Wasn't me, Ma!" Ailbhe says.

"Well that matters not." She turns to me. "Yes, dear. Your da and I feel that this is necessary, unless you want your da to lock you away forever. We nearly died! Again! We won't survive anything else happening to you. So don't accept this for yourself, do it for Da and me. We still have a pair of seven-year-olds to raise."

What am I supposed to say to that? I completely get it. My family is full of love and we are as close as flour in a barrel. I imagine they all suffered as much as me. Maybe even more. I can't imagine, as I go on with my life, them holding their breath each time I am in not in their sight, awaiting my return. That is no way for them to live. "Of course, Ma. I have no issue with the security."

Her body sags with relief and she lets out a breath. "Oh, that's a load off, dear." My mother crosses the kitchen and hugs me close to her. "You mean the world to us, Maeve. I love you all so much I could squeeze you to death." She motions for the boys and we wrap ourselves in a group hug. I missed my touchy-feely-lovey-dovey family.

"Ma, you're bonkers," Lugh says.

We stand in an embrace of four in silence for a long time. I can feel their relief, because I share it with them. We are united again. I hope that Keegan is prepared to live close to my family after we are wed, because I need them in my life. *Every day.* After the year I've had, I want to see my brothers grow into men. I want to be there for my ma and da as they grow old. I will take nothing in life for granted. I can't afford to.

"This family is strong, but we can only have it tested so much," Ma says.

As if on cue, Da calls for us from the parlor. We all make our way into the room.

"Thank you, gentlemen, for agreeing to keep an eye on me. It will be a great ease to my parents worries," I say, taking a seat across from them. They nod agreement to me.

"Maeve, Miles and Pierce will be living on the grounds. You are not to leave the grounds without at least one of them with you. That means the shops and visits to your friends, the fitness center, even on a date.

A date? I will be married soon enough. With Keegan by my side there will be no need for any bodyguards.

"They will ride with you at all times, and you will use a driver, since bloody kidnappers like to hide in cars," my da says, recalling my recent story. Anger clouds his face.

"Well that is fine. Can they drive me to Keegan's today?"

"Sure. I imagine that you would want to see him." He and ma share a look that I don't miss.

I want to ask what the look is for, but fear stops me. What if he has moved on, has a girlfriend? It has been a year. I won't let myself believe that. I am going to be his wife.

THE DRIVE to Keegan's parents is long. They live in Glasthule, which is only a stone's throw away from us, but my anticipation makes it feel like we have been in the car for a week. I remember the million times Keegan and I hopped on the DART, which is the bus that transported us around the city, and to and from each other's homes. The early years when we were just the best of friends.

I don't gaze out at the beauty around me. I can't, because I am suffocating on nerves and men. The driver, Aiden, is as big and strong as my bodyguards. Pierce is in the backseat with me, and Miles is up front with the driver. Thank goodness—for a second I thought they were going to sit on either side of me, leaving me in the middle like a child.

I am nervous and excited about seeing Keegan for the first time. If our reunion is anything like my reunion with my family, then it will be worth the wait. I have dreamt of this for a year. Being in his arms, his strong blue gaze holding mine, loving me. Keegan took after his ma's movie star looks. Blond hair, dreamy blue eyes, and perfect poreless skin. Tall, with the kind of body that food doesn't stick around and hide in. He will never have to worry about it stowing away in his belly, or on his hips. He burns it off before it fully digests. Lucky.

My mind flies back to the day he proposed.

We took a trip to London with his family. His mother always told me that I was the daughter she always wanted but never had, her career leaving her only time enough to have Keegan. The private dinner in the London Eye on the South Bank of the River Thames should have been my first clue. The river glowed a beautiful rainbow of reflections from the lights cast by the Ferris wheel. Keegan, down on his knees. He pulls the telltale Weir and Sons crimson ring box from his pocket. Tears fall from my eyes before he says a word. It was a fairy tale after that Photos of every moment of our engagement, wedding planners with us every step of the way. Our engagement photo even made it in a tabloid magazine. Being a model, I am not unfamiliar with having my picture taken, but going on a shoot is for work—it's not me, my personal self. I am just a nameless face, an unknown body selling a product.

When we round the bend to the Flanagan estate, my stomach is in knots. I have no idea if he is even home. Some parts of me hope he isn't home, because I am ill-prepared for this reunion.

"Miss, are you ready?" Miles asks, holding my door open.

I hadn't even noticed that he opened it. I take his extended hand to help me climb out of the car, and make my way toward the front door with a bodyguard flanking me on each side.

"May I help you?" the young woman who answers the door asks us. Her brogue is thick and musical. She was definitely born here. She isn't dressed like domestic staff. She is striking, with dark hair that falls heavy to her waist, and the clearest blue eyes. Perhaps she is one of Mrs. Flanagan's actor friends.

"Sure. I am here to see Keegan Flanagan."

"Who may I tell him is calling?"

"Maeve O'Malley."

Recognition lights her face. My face might not be familiar, but my name sure is. She makes space for us to enter, and I walk inside. This place has been home to me for a few years. Miles and Pierce follow me inside. I make my way to the parlor. I don't sit. I am far too nervous for that.

"I will go and fetch Keegan," she says. Her smile is brittle, her cheeks warm.

I gaze around at the familiar room. Pictures everywhere. Most of them have always been of Keegan's ma with famous actors, her receiving awards. There are pictures of my love at various ages. There are no pictures of me and him? I remember when pictures of the two of us were scattered all around the parlor. I can't find one. Perhaps with me missing, it was too hard for him, poor Keegan—*but I'm here now, my love.*

Then I see a picture, one that makes my heart drop into my stomach, and my stomach drop to my knees. It is a picture of Keegan and the beautiful girl who answered the door. I realize, as my eyes take in the room, that there are many pictures of the two of them. Horseback riding, him helping her down from the steed. My steed, Henrietta. I was the only one who rode her. She was my gift from Keegan. A picture of them on a picnic. Another on the Liffey, relaxing in a canoe. The final picture I see nearly stops my heart. It is Keegan and the girl, whose name I don't know, kissing in front of the London Eye. I am dizzy. I turn from the photo journey that is tearing my heart out.

"Are you okay, miss?" Miles asks.

"Not really," I say.

Light floods the entrance to the back door and I know that I am going to be face to face with Keegan. I want to run, but I can't. I want to jump into his arms, but I won't. I need answers.

Who is this girl, this woman?

Where do I fit into your life?

But this is his dance to lead.

"Maeve?! Is that you?" Keegan's voice bursts into the room. The smile on his face says that he is surprised, but happy to see me.

That is a good sign. Perhaps the photographs mean nothing. She could easily be someone to help him pass the time until my return.

Keegan crosses the room and wraps his arms around me. "For the love of Pete. I am so happy you are okay." He kisses my forehead. "You've no idea how I have worried. How we all have."

His words fill my heart. The woman is standing at the perimeter of the parlor. I can see from her pained expression that if she was someone for Keegan to pass the time with, she didn't see it that way. She is worried, about me. I feel for her, because I felt that way only a moment ago. Being loved by Keegan in any capacity is a gift.

"I guess I should leave you two," she says in a small voice. Her exit is dramatic. Tears spill over her eyes and she runs out of the room.

"Gemma!" Keegan calls out and runs after her.

My stomach falls again. I believe I misread the situation.

I sit on the nearest sofa and hug myself. I am at Keegan's mercy. He alone has the power here. I wait for his return. The tension is palpable. Even Miles and Pierce can feel it, because I know they want to say something. Thankfully, they don't. I shoot up from the sofa when he returns.

"Can we take a walk, Maeve?"

I nod.

He takes me by the hand. His thumb rubbing the back of my hand feels so familiar. My heart breaks for Gemma, because he must have told her it was over between them.

As we make it out the door he turns to Miles and Pierce. "I need some time alone with Maeve, please."

My bodyguards do not stop following us. "That is not possible. We were hired to be wherever Miss O'Malley is," Pierce says.

Keegan looks at me. I can see he is pleading for me to ask them to wait. Give us some privacy. "Maeve, nothing is going to happen to you with me around."

"I can't, Keegan. I promised Ma and Da that I would keep them with me at all times. They even live with us now," I tell him.

He exhales. I can see from the change in his expression that he is annoyed. He is used to getting his way, but doesn't fight this. We walk into his mother's enchanted garden—at least that is what I call it, because it is a dream garden, with every flower, root, and plant you can imagine. Vivid reds, pinks, yellows, oranges, blues, purples abound. And green, so much green. Even in one of the greenest places on earth, the enchanted garden is greener. So only magical things can happen here, and they do. This is where the pot of gold must be, but I haven't found it yet. This garden is where angels must spend their free time. I run to my favorite spot in the entire garden and sit on my tree swing. The swing itself is attached to the tree by strong vines of the most beautiful ivy, which has always baffled me. Like I said, magical. And now, in the most beautiful place I know, I am prepared to reunite with the love of my life. My reason for surviving The Chamber is standing before me.

Miles and Pierce sweep the garden for would-be threats. When they seem content that there are none, they give us a modicum of privacy, standing near the entrance. Still close enough to hear us, but I hope they can at least pretend not to.

Like the most normal thing we have ever done, Keegan walks behind me and begins to push me in the swing. We are both silent. I don't know why he is short of tongue, but I am because this is a defining moment in our relationship.

"What happened to you, Maeve?" Keegan asks, breaking the silence.

I use my feet to stop the swing. The motion is only making me dizzier. "I was kidnapped. They were waiting for me in my car when I was heading home from the fitness center."

"Who, Maeve?" He walks around to face me. "Who took you?"

"I don't know. A crazy person. He took six other girls at the same time as me. I have no idea where I was!" I begin to weep.

He takes a seat on the swing with me. "What did you do there for an entire year? Why did they release you? I mean, I am happy beyond belief that they did. I just, I don't understand."

"Use your imagination and I bet I did it," I say.

He jumps up from the swing. "I am going to be sick."

He paces.

"Are the Garda looking for this place? This psycho?" he asks.

"They are."

I get up and pace with him.

"Are you okay, Maeve?" he asks, looking at me for the first time. "I nearly died when you were gone."

Hearing that gives me hope that my prayers were answered, that he mourned me, but didn't give up on me, on us. "Thoughts of you were the only thing that kept me alive," I admit. "Keegan?" I stop pacing and face him. "Who is Gemma?"

He stops too. Almost in midstep. "Gemma. Is. My fiancée."

The air is released from my balloon.

His fiancée.

His fiancée.

Doesn't seem like he was missing me too much. I thought that title was mine. "I thought I was your fiancée."

"You are, Maeve. I mean, you were. But you were gone. What if you never came back? Was I supposed to wait for you forever? Gemma helped me to get over..."

My breathing catches on an air bubble. I nearly choke on the lump in my throat. "Me? Get over me?" I finish his sentence.

He paces back and forth before stopping in front of me again. "I suffered when you went missing. I loved you so much, I was planning on living the rest of my life with you...and one day you just vanished."

"But I'm here now." I glance over at Miles and Pierce, and I can see that they are trying very hard to pretend they are not listening. I know for a fact that they have heard every single word. "I guess I can't blame you for seeking comfort in another," I say to him. "So what now? I mean, do you love her? Do you still love me?" Bold and hard questions are never easy for me, but I can't breathe until I know that we are okay. That he is still mine.

"I love Gemma. We are to be wed in a week."

For the second time, I throw up in my mouth a little. *Did he say a week?* "And, in light of my return? Will there be any changes in your life? I guess what I mean is, what about us, Keegan? Doesn't me being here change anything, *everything*?"

"Listen, Maeve, not to sound like a total barse but life is about choices and I have made mine. I'm going to marry Gemma."

"Choices?" I raise my voice. "Choices? What choice do I get, Keegan? I was snatched off the street. I was going about my business, two weeks away from marrying the man of my dreams, when someone drugged me and made me a sex slave! I nearly died in there! The only thing keeping me alive was thoughts of you! Knowing that I would be with you again!" I couldn't stop the waterfall from coming if I wanted to. "I come home to find my life more banjaxed than ever, because you didn't have enough faith in us to wait!" I cross my arms in protection. I let my red hair fall in a heavy curtain to block him from my view, if only for a moment.

Keegan takes me by each shoulder, squaring me to look at him.

"Well thank god for that, Maeve. I'm glad I could be a beacon of strength for you while you suffered so. It's just that I have moved on. I can't be with someone like you now, knowing what you went through for an entire year. You are all used up now."

My hand connects with his face before I have a chance to stop it. Twice. My guards are near me in an instant. They don't know Keegan, and I assume they are protecting me from an equal reaction from him. He might be behaving cruelly, but I doubt he'd be cruel enough to strike me. "How dare you! Keegan, you are more than a barse. You are no gentlemen. Nothing that happened to me was my doing! And you so easily cast me away. I am a person! A person I thought *you* loved!"

He massages his jaw, his perfect skin reddened. "I guess I deserved that." He sizes up Miles and Pierce. "I don't mean to be cruel. It's just that I am meant for greatness, and I can't exactly have someone with your sordid past lurking in the darkness. Do you know what type of scandal that might create for me?"

I lunge for him again. This time Miles steps in between the two of us. "Miss, I promise you, he isn't worth it."

You know what? He is right. I wouldn't want to be with someone who thinks so little of me.

"You know what, Keegan Flanagan? You and your future can go to hell," I say and I walk away from the enchanted garden, and I don't look back. I walk to the car, my shoulders back, my head held high. I make it into the car, with the high-level security window tint, and let go. I sob for everything I lost because of The Chamber. No man will ever want me because of what happened to me there. Keegan may be no gentleman, but I am no lady either. I am just a shell.

5

*W*hat *a douche.* What real man kicks the woman he is supposed to love to the curb like this after all that she suffered? I should beat the shit out of him. When I got this assignment I almost turned it down. But I said yes as a favor to my dad. I had no idea what I was signing up for. A beautiful young woman kidnapped for an entire year, and just released. I'm not a fucking idiot either—no one needs to spell out to me what this poor girl's duties were during her year of captivity. *Damn.*

Living in Ireland, on the property. Also not something I expected, but the accommodations are good. Pierce, Aiden and I are staying in the guest house. It has three bedrooms, two bathrooms, and a full kitchen. Though I get the impression that Mrs. O'Malley likes to cook, so that too is a plus.

When I met Miss Maeve O'Malley this morning my heart broke for her. What she must have gone through. And why—because she is a beautiful girl? Sometimes beauty is a curse. One thing I have learned in the short couple of years I have done security is that I only want sons, if I have children at all. I know women are in the military and can shoot guns, and a lot of them can take care of themselves, but there are still a majority of them who can't. If I was Mr. O'Malley,

I wouldn't just hire security for my daughter. I would make sure she was lethal.

Now look at her, weeping in a tiny ball because her douchebag of an ex-fiancé thinks that he is god's gift to women and can treat her any way he wants. Sure, he moved on. I get that, but to be so cold and insensitive? What a fucking ass. Pierce and I heard everything that he said to Maeve and he deserved even more than the slap across his face. He deserves for me and Pierce to go back there after we drop off Miss O'Malley and teach him how to treat a lady. My blood boils, listening to her as she tries to silence her cries. I want to comfort her, but we are strangers too. The only thing I can do is my job and that is to make sure she gets safely from point A to point B. That is all. But I feel especially protective of her. Poor, beautiful girl.

6

MAEVE: SLOWLY DYING

I don't wait for anyone to open my door when we return home. In fact, I don't even wait for the sedan to stop. I crash through the front door, skipping two steps at a time to get to my room. There I do the only thing I can, my life spiraling out of control. The only thing I held on to for a year was a big fat lie. I sob.

I thought Keegan was my world. In my heart I believed that he could bring me back to life. If the man who is supposed to love me the most in the world doesn't want me, then no one will. I am banjanxed.

I startle when I hear a knock on my door. "Please go away!" I shout.

Ma walks in anyway. "Honey, are you okay?" She is at my side at once.

"Keegan is getting married to Gemma in a week. Apparently I'm no longer good enough for him."

Ma climbs into bed with me and holds me. "This is true, darling. You are not good enough for him."

I pull away from her embrace. "What?"

She pulls me back to her. "You are better than that. Better than good enough for him. Because if he can treat you this way, he doesn't have a good bone in his little dirtball of a body." She squeezes me.

"Oh, Ma, this isn't fair!" I wail. "What did I do to deserve these things happening to me? I have lost everything."

My ma rubs my back and lets me sob. "Fate can't be explained. Sometimes bad things happen to the best of us. We are good people, Maeve. You are a wonderful, darling girl. I will never understand why we have suffered so, but you have to be strong. We will get through this as a family."

I nod into my ma's chest. Tears hitch in my throat, causing my breathing to stutter.

"I will make you some tea."

I bury myself in my covers waiting for Ma to return. My life is in shambles. Keegan was supposed to heal me. Instead, he hurt me. I will never forgive him. Not that he cares one iota about me or how I feel about him.

I pretend to be asleep when my ma returns with tea.

The next morning I pretend to be asleep when the boys jump on my bed in an attempt to wake me for the day. I made a decision that my bed is where I plan to stay, perhaps forever. My da can save a lot of money on bodyguards since I am never leaving home again.

Well, I only manage to stay in bed until about noon because my family sucks. No one checks on me, and I know why. They are waiting me out, until I get so hungry and thirsty that I can't possibly stay in my room any longer.

A place at the table is set for me, but I don't sit down. Instead I scoop up my plate and try in vain to make a run for it.

"Don't even think about it, Maeve. You will eat your dinner with us. Now, sit," my da commands.

My shoulders sag as I obey. I sink as deep into my seat as I can, hoping that I will disappear. I slide the hood to my robe over my head to hide further. I expect my da to protest, but he doesn't. I am sure he is happy that I have made an appearance. I dig right into my stew. *So delicious.* Meat, potatoes, and veggies—a slice of heaven in my new personal hell. I spoon the amazing stew into my mouth and guzzle my milk like a prisoner trying to protect her food. I need to fill my belly and make it back to my room, because I can't handle the stares that I feel on my face from everyone. "Thanks, Ma. I always loved your stew. I'm going to bed."

They don't stop me, but their silence is a dead giveaway that they are worried about me. I'm sure they are, but after all I suffered in The Chamber I was so certain that my life back home would be something to be happy about, to make me thankful every moment that I was home. I guess it was my stupid fault for putting all of that happiness in the hands of a man.

This is how my life goes for more than two weeks. My folks refuse to bring me even a toast point. If I want food I must make my way out of my room, down the stairs and into the kitchen. Well, fine. But I am not going to dress. Each meal I drag my depressed body with all of its aches and pains down to the kitchen, wearing a thick, fluffy pink bathrobe and matching pink slippers.

My hair I don't bother to wash or comb. A greasy mess.

My face I only wash because the sleep that gathers in the corners of my eyes is uncomfortable.

My body I only wash because the smell becomes unbearable otherwise.

Personally, I don't care if I ever leave the house again. Some meals Miles and Pierce join us. I only offer a nod as a greeting. This must be the easiest gig they have ever had—a depressed recluse is easy to guard, seeing how I never leave the house. Still, my folks let me wallow in my own suffering, as long as I come down for meals, and allow them to lay eyes on me.

Things change at lunch after my routine nears the three-week mark. I drag my body back up the stairs after another delicious meal. Each step feels like climbing a mountain.

About an hour later there is a knock at my door that I have no intention of answering. I can't handle anyone telling me that I will be okay, that I will find someone else. Or worse, lying to me and telling me that I am strong. I don't want to hear any of it, because it isn't true. The person lets themselves into my room anyway, and I am surprised to see Saoirse and Ciara. The tears spill unchecked. These girls have been my best friends since my family moved to Ireland. Before they make it to my bed, they are in tears too. We fold into a big hug and cry collectively. I hadn't expected to seek them out after everything that happened with Keegan, but I am happy to see them.

"Maeve, where have you been, love?" Saoirse speaks up first.

"We thought the worst. We were sick with worry," Ciara says.

I pull the covers back and like we have so many times before we all climb into my bed. "It was the worst, I'm afraid. Me, six other girls, a lot of men, and a lot of sex," I summarize. Their collective gasps tell me how they feel. And they are wrapping me in another loving embrace. "Then there is Keegan."

"We heard. He is a mingin' eejit," Saoirse says.

"I hope he gets a fecking scorching case of knobrot," Ciara adds.

For the first time since leaving Keegan's I smile. A giggle escapes. "Maybe his lad will fall off. That's what he'll be famous for, having no lad," I say.

The image of him missing his penis makes us all burst into laughter. I needed this.

"Then again, how can such a dick be missing his lad?" I say and we laugh even louder.

The door flies open and Ma and Da are standing in the entrance. They are smiling at the three of us.

"Thanks for calling them," I say.

They don't respond. Instead they close the door behind them. I am sure the sound of laughter coming from my room after so much pain is an answered prayer.

"So are you really good at getting yar oats off, then? I bet you could teach us a thing or two," Ciara asks.

"Ciara, don't be ridiculous. What a god-awful thing to say!" Saoirse admonishes.

I blush a few shades. I mean, Ciara isn't wrong—I would consider myself highly skilled in the art of sex or *getting my oats off*, as Ciara calls it. We Irish have the most colorful slang, and my friends could teach a course on it. "Ciara is right. I mean, as awful as it sounds, I learned just about everything there is to learn about sexual pleasure," I say.

"Was it awful?" Ciara asks.

I sit up in bed and they follow, giving me their undivided attention. "It was awful about fifty percent of the time, to be truthful. The man who runs the place is quite the genius. He threatens us so that we don't try to escape, but then he treats us like royalty the whole time we are there. Well, minus the having sex with strangers. But that was the weird thing too. It was the same guys every time, so after a while they became less strangers. This whole thing makes me feel crazy. Why didn't I try to escape? Why didn't I fight back?" I process what I am saying to them because it is true. The men weren't savage or cruel. They were nice. Kinky, but nice. But that doesn't make it right. That makes it worse.

"What do you think would have happened to you if you tried to escape?" Saoirse asks. "I'll tell you," she says, not giving me a chance to respond. "You might have been hurt. Or worse, killed. You did the right thing, Maeve."

"The other girls and I decided that if a year went by and we didn't get set free as promised, then he lied and had no intentions of letting us go, and we would try to escape." We made that pact about a month in. "Doesn't matter. I will never be free. According to Keegan, I am all used up. The nightmares are insufferable, and sleep is my least favorite thing."

The look on their faces is the very look that I am coming to abhor. My ma wears it, my da wears it. And the boys, even though they are too young to even know it, they wear it. Pity.

"Well, I have just the thing for you." Ciara says, pulling out a bottle of pills. "They are called Blank Overs. You will never have a nightmare again. Take one pill to take the edge off and you will be happy and worry-free. Take two before bed and you will sleep like the angel that you are."

I take the proffered bottle and give it a look-see. They are definitely not from a legitimate doctor. Street pills. Could be dangerous. Then I consider who has given them to me and know in my heart that Ciara would never hurt me. Saoirse is the level-headed one and she isn't showing any alarm in regards to the pills. I open the lid and pop a pill into my mouth. I snap the lid back into place and put the bottle in my nightstand.

"That should last you about a month or two."

I nod. I'm not one to take pills but I have to do something before my parents have me committed for depression.

It is too soon before the girls have to leave. But not without setting a girls night in a couple of days.

THE BLANK OVERS did their job for sure, because about half an hour after taking just one I was hopping out of bed, grabbing a quick wash-up in the shower, and heading down the stairs. I needed to get out of this house.

"Ma! Da!" I yell through the house on my way to the kitchen. I don't see anyone so I continue to yell. "Ma! Da!"

My folks come running from the parlor, worry covering their faces. "What is it, love?" Ma says.

"Where are Miles and Pierce? I want to get out of the house," I say.

I don't miss the glance they exchange. "Pierce has gone into town on an errand, seeing as you never planned to leave the house again. I will fetch Miles at once," Da says.

THE DRIVER PULLS the sedan in front of the house. Miles opens the door for me and I slide in. He slides into the back seat with me. "The Coffee House, please, Aiden," I instruct the driver, who I secretly think my folks planted as a third bodyguard. No way a guy with that many muscles is only driving the car.

The car ride is quiet. I am full of excited energy and I fidget in an effort to release some of it. When we pull up to the coffee shop, Aiden waits in the car, while Miles and I head inside. It is a rainy day in April, with loads of fog just like I like.

I turn to him. "How do you take your coffee?"

"Two creams, two sugars," he says.

I buy his coffee and mine and motion for us to take a seat at an empty table. He looks uncomfortable with the idea, but I don't let him say no.

"Where are you from?" I ask when we settle into our seats.

"Military brat, so a bit of everywhere," he says.

I take a sip of my coffee. "Thanks for looking out for me," I say.

He offers me a soft smile and nods. I know it's his job, but I like that he doesn't feel the need to tell me so. "Hey, I'm sorry about what happened with the douche. I can't remember his name so that is what I will call him, if that is okay with you."

"It's fitting."

We don't say much else for a while, but the silence is killing me. I know this is not a date. He is doing his job. Which explains why his head seems to be on a swivel, always assessing.

"How old are you, Miles?"

"Twenty-five," he says. All business.

"Listen, I know you are here to do a job, to keep me safe. I don't know, I have no one to talk to. I just thought..."

"I'm sorry for being so distant. I think it's for the best though, because if we became friends, it would make it very hard to protect you, Miss O'Malley."

"Maeve. Please just call me Maeve," I say.

"Fine then, Maeve. When I took the job I had no idea that you would be so beautiful, and you are in a very vulnerable place in your life. The more friendly and acquainted we become, the harder it is to keep you safe. I drop my guard once and that could mean your safety. We need to keep things professional. Deal?"

The smile that crosses my face is one I couldn't suppress if I wanted to. Until this moment I hadn't considered my bodyguard as anything but that. Looking at him now, I see that he is so much more than that. He is damn hot. Brown skin that is creamy and smooth.

Brown eyes too, but with a depth to them that takes you in and traps you. And his body—well, damn. He is sculpted perfection, stashed in over six feet of muscled body. Maybe it's the Blank Over that is making me behave this way. But I like it. I never considered dating someone from another race. Not that I cared—our folks always taught us that a person isn't their color; the skin is just the covering for the soul inside.

Hell, look at Keegan, blond and blue, covering the devil himself. "Deal."

But he's right, we should keep this professional.

"Thanks for the coffee," he says.

"Welcome."

We make it to the car but I am still not ready to go back home. "Can we check out some good old Dublin *craic* before we head back?"

He nods.

The driver takes us to the Temple Bar District. We don't walk into any pubs. Instead, we walk around and I people-watch. I could get lost in the small crowd of people. It feels liberating and for the first time I feel free. Nameless faces who don't know me, don't know what I've been through. To them I could be anyone. I twirl a couple of times, arms out at my sides, my face to the heavens. Miles watches me carefully, while watching everyone else.

"Maeve! Is that you?" A voice calls from behind us.

I turn to the voice, noting Miles's protective stance, leaving nothing to chance. "Oh my goodness, Ronan!"

He wraps me into a tight hug. I can feel the tension from Miles, who is not happy with the contact. It's not like Ronan is going to sink a knife into my gut while he is hugging me, but I guess Miles doesn't know that. All he knows is that he is protecting the most unfortunate girl on this planet.

We separate and I hear Miles let out a breath.

"Where have you been, love? You vanished into thin air!"

I choose not to answer his question. "This is Miles." I introduce them and they shake hands. Of course they size each other up, as if there is a reason to. "Ronan and I went to high school together," I tell Miles.

"How have you been?" Ronan asks.

"Fine. Good."

"Keegan? How is he?" he asks before obviously swapping glances between Miles and I.

Can you say *gut punch, kick in the balls*, if I had them. "We broke up." I look down. The Blank Overs suddenly ooze out of my system at the mention of Keegan's name. I will have to remember to carry them with me. In a flash flood, I remember everything I was doing so well at forgetting, and I am no longer on the *craic*-filled streets of my beloved Dublin, but in the enchanted garden with Keegan, getting my heart ripped out. I vaguely hear Miles say something about Keegan being a douche and excusing ourselves. We turn to walk. Well, Miles does. I can't seem to make my feet move.

"Are you okay?" he asks.

Hot tears blaze down my cheeks, tears of pain and shame, because I know what this means as I remember. "No man will ever want me after what I have been through. I might as well join a convent because I am used and damaged. I didn't ask for this, Miles."

He breaks the rules and wraps me in a caring embrace. He holds me for what feels like forever, right in the center of the sidewalk, forcing people to walk around us. "You are beautiful and, from what I can see, smart. And no man should blame you for something beyond your control. If any man judges you for that, then he is not a man. He is a fool. You deserve the world. God knows you have been through enough, and I will never let anything happen to you again," he promises.

I nod repeatedly. I walk with him toward the car. His arm is around me, but not in a romantic way, for support. I am not exactly sure-footed at the moment. When Aiden sees us he exits the car immediately. I guess Miles's arms around me indicates a problem.

"Miles?" He glances around with alert eyes. I knew he wasn't just a driver.

"Everything is fine. Just an unexpected run-in with an old friend," he says.

I ease myself into the back of the sedan. Miles gets in on the other side. Again, I fold myself into the tiniest ball I can manage. I want to disappear. I know that Miles said I am deserving and that there is a man out there who won't judge me, but what if I never find him?

I must fall asleep on the way back home because I am awakened to Miles tapping me. I don't speak. Instead I unfold and drag myself out of the car. "Thanks," I say in his direction.

"Don't mention it," he says and follows me to the front door. He comes inside with me, always working, but I guess if kidnappers can break into my car and wait for me, they can certainly be waiting in an empty house.

When we cross the threshold we learn that mine is full. *Great.* My grandparents on my mother's side, Ma's sisters and my da's brother are all inside waiting for me. *Why are they all here?*

"Maeve!" Someone shouts and all heads turn toward me. I freeze.

Within seconds I am being passed around and hugged in a barrage of loving family members. We are a lovey, touchy brood. I manage to get through all of them before I excuse myself to my room, my excuse that I need to grab something. Not a lie. I need to take another Blanko, which is what I have decided to call them. I am in near panic by the time I reach my room. I am not ready for a home-coming party. What have my parents told them about my disappear-ance? *I can't.* I pop a Blanko and wait for it to kick in. Of course there is a knock at my door. And just like a true family member of mine they don't wait for me to answer or give them permission. It's my Aunt Karen, Ma's youngest sister.

"Sorry to disturb you, love, but I wanted a chance to tell you how much I love you, dear. If you ever need anything or someone to talk to, you call me anytime, you hear?" she says. She turns to leave after saying her piece.

"Would you have tried to escape? Am I an idiot because I didn't?" I can't bring myself to look her in the eyes. This is the question I fear everyone who finds out what happened to me is going to ask. "I mean, for an entire year I stayed and obeyed, in hopes that I would be released as promised, but I never tried to leave. He said if we tried to leave he wouldn't hurt us, you see. He said he would hurt our families, but I think people are going to judge me for not trying to fight back or escape."

She makes her way back to me and takes a seat on my bed, gesturing for me to sit with her. I follow her and sit. My auntie scoots in very close. She looks so much like my ma and me—fair, freckled skin, thin build, green eyes. The only difference is her red hair is curly. "I want you ta listen ta me, Maeve…everybody wants to poke around in yar head and tell you what you should've done, but not a one of them has been through half of what you have, you hearin' me? Of course they can say you should've escaped, but until they are sittin' there faced with the same decision as you were, they can't say shite, you hear, not a damn word about it!" Her face is red with anger. "Remember my BASE jumping fiasco?"

I nod and giggle. We were all there with video cameras, ready to film her epic adventure.

"I wanted to do it so bad. It looked so liberatin' and freein', until I made it to the jump site and nearly shat me pants… Looks a lot different when it's staring you in the face. You tell em' I said so. You'll be alright, my love. You're stronger than you give yarself credit for. I know because my blood flows through yar veins. Now, I'm gonna leave you, and I'm gonna announce downstairs if one bloody fecker says a word to you about why you didn't this or didn't that, I'm gonna knock their lights out!" She kisses my forehead and walks out the door.

I can only smile at the thought of Karen beating someone up. If anyone would do it, she would. She says I am strong like her. I wish that were true.

It takes about twenty minutes for the Blanko to kick in. When it does, I make my way down the stairs to mingle with my family. Miles and Pierce are never far. Pierce spends most of his time assessing the room, while Miles spends his watching me. The attraction I feel toward him is palpable.

I wish I'd had access to these pills when I was in The Chamber. It would have been nothing. I feel amazing, like I can conquer the world. As a matter of fact, I know I can. First place I want to start is by calling my dipshit ex-fiancé. I politely excuse myself and make my way into Da's office. I pick up the phone and dial his cell—I know it by heart, of course.

Ring, ring, ring. "Hello?" Keegan answers.

His voice shouldn't bring about the emotional feelings that it does, but it does. I have held on for a year to the idea of him comforting me when I returned home. The idea of his voice soothing me when a nightmare claimed my sleep.

"Hello?" he repeats.

"It's me."

"Maeve?"

"Yes."

"Why are you calling me?"

"Just to talk."

"What is left to discuss? I thought you understood."

"I thought that maybe after a couple of weeks you would have time to reconsider."

There is a long pause on the other line. I wait for him to respond.

"If I haven't tried to reach out to you in as much time, I would think that it was obvious I have not reconsidered anything. Please don't call me anymore."

The line goes dead.

It really is over. I plop down on Da's office chair. This time I don't cry. The Blanko seems to protect me from the pain, from reality.

"You okay?"

I look up to find Miles standing in the doorway.

I shake my head. I am anything but okay. It is a tough pill to swallow when you realize that the guy you thought hung the moon is actually cruel and unfeeling.

"May I?" he asks, gesturing to the seat across from the desk.

I nod.

I dare a look up at him. He is gazing into my eyes, but they aren't expecting. "You must think I'm an idiot for calling him. I knew it was over before I called, but I needed to see for myself if he really meant it."

"You'll get no judgment from me. I am not in your shoes, so it's not my place to say what you should do or how you should feel."

Sounds like he has been talking to Karen. "Thanks."

We sit in silence for a long time, but not uncomfortable silence. This is peaceful silence. Safe and peaceful.

I break it anyway. "How did you find yourself in this business? With your looks you could be a model or an actor," I say.

He breaks a smile and a small laugh escapes his very soft, full lips. "Thank you for the compliment, but acting and modeling have never been an aspiration of mine. I mentioned that I grew up in a military family. My older brother is a Marine, my younger brother is an Airman. My father spent most of his career in the Marines too, but retired and fell into high-level security—politicians and dignitaries. That is how he met your da, as you call him. They have been friends for some years. After six years in the Marines, I joined him protecting important people. For the past two years I have protected a couple princesses, a prince, a few high-profile celebrities, and now you. I believe you fall into the category of royalty." He smiles.

Oh, that is a heart-melting smile. Deep dimples make his handsome face more so. Any girl would be lucky to be on the receiving end of a smile like that.

"Well, my claim is pretty far down the line. It's hardly worth mentioning or adding to my resume," I admit.

I can't help the warm blush that accompanies the smile that is plastered across my face. He smiles back at me. Why are we two goofballs?

"You have a beautiful smile, Maeve. I wish you felt good enough to do it more. I want that for you."

"Me too."

"So your parents say you grew up in the States," he says.

"Yep, until age ten. That's why my accent isn't as strong as everyone else in the family. My folks and the boys were all born here.

I was born in New York. My ma hadn't planned on me being born in the U.S. but I came a month earlier than expected, so there wasn't really a choice. Dual citizenship has its perks. We lived in New York, D.C., and California. My da did foreign-relations-type stuff. I even went to a couple American private schools. Did they tell you what happened to me, why we moved back here?"

Miles shakes his head. "They were vague. Just that you had suffered a tragedy when you were a young girl," he says.

"I'm not surprised they didn't tell you. Da blames himself. I was nine when it happened," I say.

"You don't have to tell me if you don't want to. I understand," he says.

"I think I do."

Miles stands up. He picks up the chair he was sitting in and brings it around to where I am. His close proximity is comforting.

"I was in grade school, grade four to be exact. The bell rang for the end of the day and I walked out to my family's SUV. It was parked in the usual spot. I opened the door and hopped in just like I would on any other school day, and said hi to our driver Samuel, only it wasn't him. I don't know what happened to Samuel, but he wasn't driving our car. The doors made that locking sound. I tried to open the back door but it wouldn't budge. I may have been nine but I knew something was wrong. Long story short, I was taken for ransom. I wasn't hurt, per se. My mouth was taped, I was tied up and blind-folded. I was scared to death. I was with the kidnappers for five days, before my da traded me for money. We moved here soon after. My folks felt like I would be safer at home. Turns out nowhere on earth is safe for me. So when I was taken a second time, well my folks weren't taking any risk of it happening a third time. That's why I have you. Well, you and Pierce...and Aiden."

He smirks and nods at my recognition of Aiden as a bodyguard too. "I'm sorry," he says.

"It's just my unfortunate luck," I say.

"There is a saying I use a lot. 'Luck favors the prepared.' Maeve, the things that have happened to you don't mean you are lucky or unlucky. It just means you were in a situation you weren't prepared to deal with. I think it's great that your dad hired us, but I also think you should be able to protect yourself. Stand up."

I do.

"Turn away from me."

I do.

He grabs me from behind, just like a kidnapper might—arm around my neck and hand covering my mouth. "Break free."

I stand there for a full minute, distracted by the feel of his body so close to mine. He smells divine, an earthy, musky scent that works in perfect blend with his skin. His skin is warm and inviting. Being pressed up against his chiseled form is so much better than seeing it. I remember the task at hand and begin to wiggle free. Well, try to, to no avail. He lets me go.

"What happened?" he asked.

I turn to face him. "I couldn't get free. You are too strong," I protest.

"Strength actually has nothing to do with it. Next time, you have to react the second you feel me grab you because that is your best opportunity, before I have a chance to secure my grasp on you. You are going to step out to the side with your right leg like this." He steps out wide with one. I can't tell if it's his right or left leg because I am facing him, and that always confuses me. "At the same time, lean forward in one move. I will be off balance and I will flip over and fall, giving you a chance to run. Later I will teach you how to defend yourself so you don't have to run, but until you master the basics that is your best bet. Do you want to continue?"

I nod.

We move from behind the desk and into the center of the office for more room.

Miles begins to place me into the hold once again. I focus my energy not on his close proximity, but the task at hand, and before he can grasp onto me completely, two things happen. The door to the office swings open and Miles goes flying over my shoulder, landing onto his back with a loud thud.

I did it!

"What is the meaning of this?" Da shouts. I'm sure it looks much worse than it is.

Miles hops up. We are both embarrassed. "Miles was showing me how to get out of a hold if someone grabs me from behind. Self-defense, Da," I say.

"She is a natural, sir," Miles says.

Da looks back and forth between Miles and me as if he is not sure what to believe. "Well, then. Carry on," he says. He walks out the door, closing it behind him, then swiftly opening it back, all the way.

Message received.

"Thanks, Miles. I think I will hit the hay, but I would love to try some of this again," I say, punching the air in celebration for successfully flipping him onto the ground. "I am a natural."

Miles laughs at my display. "Deal."

I feel his eyes on me as I make my way out of the office.

I say goodnight to my family, who will most likely be here when I wake up in the morning, Irish whiskey putting them on their backs for sure. No surprise. Us Irish don't need an excuse to party. I pop another Blanko and fall into my bed. I think I am asleep before my head hits the pillow. I dream.

I am in The Chamber. It is midweek and my groomer has just finished preparing me for the men who will have me tonight. I am dressed in a beautiful jade green gown that shimmers. From behind it appears to be any normal ball gown, full with layers underneath. But it tells a different story from the front because the fabric doesn't connect. Instead, it is held together by three carefully appointed ribbons tied into bows across my chest and stomach. Everything is exposed. The stranger tells me to stand by the bed. I follow his command, my eyes closed because I don't want to see who is coming for me. I don't even open them when I feel hot lips attach to my nipple, sucking and licking. The stranger quickly goes to work on the ribbons, pushing the gown off my shoulders, and the gown falls in a puddle on the floor. A warm hand cups my sex and gives it a soft squeeze before two fingers slip inside me. Steadily in and out the fingers move, while the mouth finds my other nipple and begins sucking. The motion inside me begins to stir feelings deep in the pit of my belly. I don't want it to feel good but it does. I am guided to sit on the edge of the bed, and feel the presence of a cock wanting to enter my mouth. My eyes still closed, I take it into my mouth and suck. It is warm and salty and thick. I suck and lick the entire length, hearing moans of delight from the stranger.

When he is satisfied, he lays me down on the bed and instructs me to move back. I do. With my eyes still closed, I feel his breath upon my face, the warmth of his body over me. This isn't my first night in The Chamber, and I've learned that if I close my eyes, I can pretend this is anyone I want it to be.

"Open your eyes and look at me." The voice is kind and familiar.

When I open my eyes the stranger who isn't a stranger sinks his cock deep inside me. It is Miles. Oh. This changes everything. When I glance around, we are not in The Chamber but my bedroom at home. I wrap my arms around his neck and pull his face to mine, kissing him deeply, thanking him for every thrust inside me. I tilt my hips up greedily to get more of him. Over and over he pushes deep inside me. It is heaven. I build and build with each thrust, as his brown skin and my ivory become a blend of one. We both come apart at the seams together, crying out each other's names.

I wake up alone in my dark room. "Whew, well that wasn't a nightmare," I say into the air. I am surprised to dream about Miles, especially a dream like that. Now I am going to blush around him.

7

MILES: BLURRING THE LINES

I have officially crossed a line. It has nothing to do with any interaction I had with Maeve because the entire night I was professional, on my best behavior. The problem is how I felt about our interactions. When we were in the coffee shop, in complete silence, I felt something. It was looking into her eyes and seeing her pain. Then the protection I felt when she bumped into her friend on the street. Of course, I am supposed to protect her, but feeling protective of her this way is so much more personal. I know I have only known her for a few weeks, but she is in my system somehow and I can't shake her. I don't know if this is a damsel-in-distress scenario, but I can't let myself fall for her. It would jeopardize my protection detail. If I can't protect her then I shouldn't be here. I have never fallen for the damsel before and I can't start now.

I knew I was in trouble when I watched her walk toward her father's office last night. There was really no reason for me to follow her—she was home and she was safe. But that didn't stop me. I was compelled to follow. For whatever reason is driving me, I don't want her to be sad anymore. She is so sad. And then I learned that not once, but twice in her life she was taken against her will. It's not my job to save her or put a smile on her face, but for some reason that I can't explain, I want it to be.

I am startled by a knock at the guest house door. Too deep in thought. Caught off guard. Not good. I open the door to find Mr. O'Malley on the other side of it. "Sir," I say.

"May I come in, Miles?"

"Of course," I say. It is his house. "Have a seat anywhere," I add.

He clears his throat. He doesn't sit. Not good. "I wanted to speak with you personally about Maeve."

"Okay." *Shit.*

"You know your da and I go way back. I trust him with my life and he trusts you, so I will too...but I know how you youngsters get along with your flirting and your instant gratification, and all that. And, well, I want you to tread lightly because my daughter has been through a great deal. It would be natural for her to grow an attachment to her protector, but I can't have her gettin' hurt again. So you just keep it professional between you two, okay?"

"Yes, sir, I completely understand. Last night I was really teaching her self-defense moves," I clarify.

He assesses me and shoves his hands into his pockets. "That may be true, but I saw how my daughter looked at you, the blush in her cheeks. She fancies you, lad, and I want you ta know it so you don't go crossin' any professional lines," he says.

"Understood, sir."

He leaves as quick as he came.

"Well that wasn't awkward at all," I say under my breath.

She fancies me?

I'm fancied?

Nice.

8

MAEVE: MIND NUMBING

I pop two Blankos when I wake up. After a week of taking them, I find that with the level of trauma I am trying to bury, two pills at a time is the minimum to get through a day in my life. You know, be prepared for any surprises. I need to call Ciara and find out how many of these is safe to take because I am up to six a day so far. At this rate, my two-month supply won't last a month. I don't care. I will get more because they are the equivalent of a counselor in a bottle. Whatever synthetic compound is present in them and coursing through my veins just may be the key to me surviving this ordeal.

It's been a week since our impromptu family party. I know it is false confidence and joy, but I don't care—I am ready to venture out. Ciara and Saoirse are overjoyed when I ask to meet them for supper tonight. My folks are happy that I am hanging with my friends, and the twins want to tag along. I really can't believe what has become of my life. I should be on my honeymoon with Keegan right now. Instead I heard he just returned from his long honeymoon with Gemma.

When Mason kidnapped me, he ruined everything in my life. He took everything from me.

I hop in the shower and clean up before I go out. My mind drifts from Keegan to Miles. I haven't known him very long but I can see that he is an awesome guy. But I know that I can't mistake his concern for me as anything more than what he was hired to do. But I can't help it—I dreamt of Miles again last night. That makes three dreams in a week. This one wasn't sexual at all. We were in love and we were spending the day on the beach, enjoying being in each other's arms. In my dream with him I was safe, I was loved. That dream was everything. I would take a dream—wrapped in his arms, in the throes of passion, or simply sharing space—to my nightmares any night.

It doesn't take my stick-straight hair long to dry. I don a fitted sky blue dress with long, sheer sleeves, and a pair of matching heels, and I am ushered into a car with Miles in back with me.

"Good evening," he says and gives me a sideways smile. "You look very pretty," he mouths.

"Evening, and thank you," I say back. I can't help the warmth that comes to my cheeks and know that there is color there as my dream flashes into my mind.

"You sure are in a good mood," he says low enough for me to hear.

"Had an amazing dream last night," I say and I boldly gaze into his eyes, before I lose my brazenness and look away.

"Any dream that put that smile on your face must have been pretty good."

If you only knew, Miles. You were its star. If my boldest dream were my real life we would be alone in the backseat of this sedan and I would be straddling you, showing you the highlight reel.

Pierce takes his place in the passenger seat. He immediately gives his attention to us in the backseat. "What are you two going on about?"

"Nothing, Mae—I mean, Miss O'Malley was just telling me she is happy because she had a good dream."

I cut in. "It was a refreshing change to the nightmares I've been having."

Satisfied, Pierce turns to face forward in his seat.

I shoot the girls a text that I am on my way.

The restaurant Chapter One is an amazing fine dining establishment, and though I love my ma's home cooking, I can't wait to sink my teeth into the chef's mouthwatering dishes. We make it to Parnell Square in record time. Aiden lets us off at the curb and heads out to find a place to park. Inside, the maître d' takes my coat. I catch Miles as his eyes roam over me from head to toe, but I am careful not to meet them because I don't want him to feel embarrassed for being caught checking me out.

The four of us follow a young, beautiful hostess toward the back and I am delighted to see that Ciara and Saoirse reserved The Demi Salle area for tonight. Semiprivate, with room for sixteen. Located in the back of the restaurant, we are somewhat secluded from the other diners, but equally visible. I am sure that this gives the gentlemen assigned to protect me some relief. Maybe they can even relax and enjoy themselves. The room itself is gorgeous, with leather and coffee-color furnishings appointing a banquet-sized table. The girls have already arrived and the second they see me they run squealing in my direction.

"Maeve! Maeve!" They both shout in unison.

The three of us jump up and down in a huddle. "This is so pretty. I heard the food is amazing!" I say with excitement. When we separate I introduce them to my security. "This is Aiden, Pierce, and Miles. They are in charge of making sure I don't get nabbed again. These are my best girls, Saoirse and Ciara."

My girls, being the giddy young women they are, wrap each of them in a warm hug, taking all three of them by surprise.

"Okay, then," Pierce says. "We will sit down here. Right at the entrance," Pierce says, and the three of them take a seat at the end of the very large banquet-style table, while we make our way to the opposite end. I feel very safe because the only way to reach me is through three very large and skilled men.

"So, how does it feel traveling around with three gorgeous blokes?" Ciara asks.

"Come on, Cee. Only one of them could be classified as gorgeous and that is the very dashing black gentleman. Miles? Is that what you said his name is? He is to die for!" Saoirse giggles. "The other two are handsome in that avuncular sort of way." Referring to Aiden and Pierce.

"What is the story with Miles? Are you tapping that? 'Cause I would be, especially after what you've been through, Maeve," Ciara says. "What is the saying? Best way to get over a man is to get under a new one," she says in a hushed tone, but I wouldn't be surprised if Miles heard her.

Saoirse and I shake our heads.

I glance down at the table, and of course Miles is looking at me. He is always watching me. He really is a specimen. Even in his suit you can see that he has the body of an athlete. But I know firsthand that he does because my recent memories are of my body pressed against his. I'm not a fool. I am not going to jump into a relationship with the first gorgeous guy who pays attention to me, but it feels good to have a gorgeous man who knows what I've been through express any interest in me.

"Nope. We are just friends and barely that. He is here to protect me, not seduce me," I say, though the idea has potential. If he makes love like he did in my dream, I think he could erase my pain.

The waiter comes to our table bringing water with lemon for each of us. "We are all going to be having the chef's four-course meal," Saoirse says.

The waiter starts with us ladies. I order feta cheese mousse, smoked haddock, Hereford prime striploin of beef, and pumpkin cream. I am so excited for my food to arrive. The girls and I order a bottle of twelve-year-old Jameson with every intention of drinking the entire bottle. As soon as the bottle hits the table we do a round of shots. My security team watches us with no emotion. Business.

"What have I missed this past year?"

"Nothing. A fat lot of nothing, love. Saoirse and I have been living quite gregariously on our families' loot. My ma says I need to get my arse in school or I'm getting cut off. Of course, my da would never go for his only daughter being penniless, so good luck with that, Ma!"

Ciara shouts at no one. "Right now life is one big party, especially now that our girl is back. Let's toast!"

"With shots? That's rubbish. You toast with champagne," I say, giggling, the first shot of whiskey already warming me on the inside.

"You can toast with any fecking thing you want. Raise your bloody glasses!" Ciara yells.

She's right. We fill our shot glasses and hold them up, making sure they all touch. "To second chances at life," Ciara says. We clink glasses, but we don't drink because there is no way she is finished. "To getting rid of fecking douchebag ex-fiancés who don't have the brains god gave a fecking goldfish, may his fecking lad fall off!"

We attempt to take our shots.

"I'm not finished! My word, you two are a couple of boozy broads!" We burst out in the giggles again. "And lastly," she eyes us as she informs us this is the end of our toast, "may our girl Maeve find happiness in the arms of a handsome and muscular man who shall remain nameless!" Then she nods her head toward the end of the table where Pierce, Aiden, and Miles are sitting.

"Ciara!" I don't dare turn to look at Miles. I am too embarrassed. Ciara is not known for her subtlety and she made sure everyone at our table heard her.

We guzzle our shots and I pour another one as fast as I can. I need to feel numb and now, because I have a feeling my girls plan to embarrass the shite out of me.

After four shots I am good and numb. "Hey, before I can't string my words together I need more Blankos, I mean outs. They are amazing."

"Are you out already?" Saoirse says, her eyebrows raised in question.

"Don't get your panties in a wad. I still have some, but I don't think they will last two months. They are a-fecking-mazing!"

"No worries, love, I got you," Ciara says.

I catch Saoirse's worried glances a couple of times. She is definitely the more sensible one in our little group.

I take a gander down the table to Miles. He and the other guys are drinking soda of some sort—it is clear. Of course, they can't drink on the job. Miles is having a quiet conversation with Pierce, while Aiden is looking around. I manage a smile in Miles's direction and he returns it. Deep dimples adorn each cheek. God, he really is beautiful.

Our first course comes and I dig right in. Beetroot is my favorite—it's an acquired taste. *Mmm.* Our second course is laid in front of us before I finish the first. Looks like Miles went for the duck. I will have to catalog that for the future.

What?

"You have got to be fecking kidding me!" A deep, booming voice interrupts our enjoyment. A voice I recognize. I look in the direction of the noise and find Keegan and Gemma standing at the entrance of our small room. "There has got to be some fecking law for stalking, Maeve. First yar callin' me and now you are followin' me!"

I am shocked. He thinks I came here because he would be here? What's worse is he is loud about his accusations. I attempt to inform him that he is incorrect. "I had no idea—"

He cuts me off, anger coloring his face. I never noticed him being so tempered before. I knew he stopped loving me, but now I'm fairly sure that he absolutely despises me.

"Can it, Maeve. I told you it's over and I mean it! Don't make me invite the Garda."

Miles jumps up, Pierce jumps up, followed by Aiden. The three of them block my view of Keegan. Thank god.

"Just walk away, sir," Pierce says.

"He is no sir." Ciara hops up and heads toward Keegan. "I hope your lad falls off, you rancid sack of monkey shite!" Ciara yells.

"I will do no such thing! I want the Garda here to file a stalking complaint on Maeve O'Malley!" he shouts.

Something comes over me and I lose it. I get up from my seat and stand on my chair so that I can see him over my guards. "No one is following you, Keegan! You must be some kind of twit if you think you are the only one to come to this restaurant. I got your message loud and clear so leave me the hell alone!" My girls help me down when I have said my piece.

Why is he here, ruining my fun night out? He should be holding me, making me whole again. Instead he treats me like spoiled milk. Maybe that is what I am.

My girls wrap me in a huge embrace. Sobs escape me even when I don't want them to. Ciara sends him a continuous flip off.

"Oh yeah, Maeve, well I'm married to Gemma now and she doesn't appreciate some used-up skank of a whore stalking her husband!"

The next thing that happens will be in my playback reel. Miles knocks the sweet molasses out of Keegan, sending him to the ground.

"Say another unsettling word about Maeve and you will be eating through a straw. She didn't ask for the things that happened to her and you will apologize for your ignorant outburst!" Miles's voice is full of angry bass that I have never heard before. Keegan deserved no less.

"I'm not apologizing to her. I have a mind to tell everyone I know all about the new and unimproved Maeve O'Malley." A maniacal laugh escapes his lips like he discovered a grand plan to ruin my reputation.

This time Pierce snatches Keegan from the floor and pulls him really close. I can see Gemma from this vantage point and she is visibly shaken up. "Sir, I guarantee if you say another dishonorable word about Ms. O'Malley, you will be adding a catheter to the wired jaw. Our protection not only protects her from physical harm, it extends to verbal attacks from asswads like yourself. Now I don't know what arrogant tree you climbed down from, but I chose this restaurant because the chef is a good friend of mine, and I assure you I am not stalking you. If I were to chose the company of men, and I do not, I would chose a gentleman. And you, sir, I am sure have been told all your life that you are no gentleman. Now leave us." Pierce tosses him and Keegan stumbles backward.

He composes himself before walking away, making sure to glare at me as if I just became enemy number one. Why is it when someone does something wrong and gets called on it they are so mad, when they are only receiving the consequences of their poor actions? Like in action movies—the bad guys loses an important member of his crew while they are committing a *crime,* and they vow revenge. *Uh, really?*

"I am not hungry anymore," I say. "I wanna go home."

I think my girls feel the same way.

Miles makes his way down to me and sits in the empty seat next to mine. "You can't leave, Maeve."

"Why?"

"Because you will be giving that asshole exactly what he wants. He wants you scared and embarrassed. I can't have you feeling either of those things. I'm not gonna let anything happen to you or your friends." He glances over at the girls. "None of us are. So please enjoy your meal and your whiskey. Fuck him, or as you Irish say, feck him," he says.

"If only."

I don't say another word to Miles. Nor do I make eye contact with him because my weakness is my shame. If only I didn't love Keegan, it wouldn't hurt so badly the way he treats me. If I was over him or if I could bring myself to hate him, then I could stay. Instead, his words sting and burn me. Coming from the man I still love, the man who was my savior while I was in The Chamber, those words seep into my soul. I am a worthless, used-up skank. I don't hate Keegan. I really wish I could hate him. Instead, the person I do hate is myself.

My girls stand when I do and follow me toward the entrance of our private area. Aiden disappears, to no doubt pay for our unfinished meal, while the rest of us file out. Like the imbecile I must be, I glance around the room and am rewarded with Keegan doing the crying motion with his hands grinding his eyes, teasing me, followed by him waving with a huge grin plastered on his face. Seeing that, I quicken my pace, and nearly dive into the backseat of the awaiting car.

I am too ashamed to look at anyone. I don't say goodbye to my girls either. Nothing matters. How am I supposed to move forward when I have nothing? I curl into what is becoming my usual—a tiny ball—and attempt to hide the fact that I am crying. Of course, the sobs that escape around the hiccups don't help my case.

The second we arrive home I make a mad dash from the car, through my front door, and up my stairs, slamming my room door behind me.

I want to hate Keegan so much.

I want to stop loving him.

I want to stop wishing I was Gemma.

But I can't. He had a year to move on without me, while all I wished for during my year of captivity was to be in his arms. And I am supposed to just turn it off in an instant?

My love and affection?

My pain?

Well, forgive me for not being made of steel. He was the only thought that kept me strong while I was in The Chamber. Not my family, not my friends. I mean, sure I thought about them too, but I never imagined they would save me. That responsibility I gave to Keegan. What a fool I was. I put my entire life in his hands.

I know exactly what I need. I need to forget, and I know exactly what will help me forget everything. Blankos. Maybe if I am lucky and take enough of them I will never remember again. I grab them out of my drawer and cross my room to my bathroom. I stare at myself in the mirror.

Are you this weak, Maeve, over a boy? These things happen to every- one! People get dumped all the time. Green eyes stare back at me. The pain in them wrenches my heart. "Yeah, well, I have had my share of fecked-upness to last my entire life and truth be told, I'm fecking tired of all of it. I'm shit-damn-fecking tired of being me. I wish being dumped was the worst of it." I turn the faucet on and fill my glass with water, open the bottle and take every single pill inside. "Does everybody get kidnapped twice? I'll answer that question, no!" I don't know how many there are—at least twenty, thirty. "Does everybody spend a year as a fecking sex slave? The answer to that is a big, feck-ing, whopping no too!" I don't know why my subconscious is trying to talk me out of this. It isn't like it helped me to forget my life either. "So, I will take my own life into my own hands, and maybe I can finally get some fecking peace."

Now that that is done. I make my way to my desk and pull out a tablet and pen.

To my dearest family,

I am so sorry that it has come to this. The pain of living this life has proven to be too much for me to endure. I can't stand a single second more of life in this body. If I come back I hope to be a butterfly or a beautiful bird, because being a human has proven too much. I love you Ma, Da, Lugh, and Ailbhe so much. I am sorry I wasn't strong enough to stay with you.

Love forever,

Maeve

BY THE TIME I get to the salutation I have nearly ruined the note with my tears. They will be so sad. They will miss me so much, and I will forever be sorry that I couldn't stay around for them. But they aren't in my skin. That is my unfortunate burden, and I tried to return to my life and make it work. I returned from one tragedy to endure another one. Everywhere I turn in this life is pain, and to be honest I am exhausted. I can't please anyone, including myself. I've been home an entire month and nothing has changed. It hasn't gotten better. I will never bounce back. This way my family will mourn the loss of me, rather than watch me slowly wither and die. This way is much better for all of us.

The Blankos are starting to take over. I can tell because my head is light and I feel no pressure, no sadness, only peace. *Perfect peace.* I lie down on my bed and let them do their work.

I'm floating.

Gently floating on a breeze.

My body is weightless.

Happiness.

I can't feel my fingers or my toes. I try to move my fingers but I can't tell if I am successful.

There is no pain.

I no longer feel regret.

There is no fear.

No failure.

No suffering.

I only feel joy at this moment. Relief that my horrible, calamitous life is coming to an end. My family will never have to suffer worrying about me again. They can remember me however they want, whatever will bring them the most peace. They don't have to pretend they aren't scared to death anymore. They too will finally know peace. My folks deserve to be happy, something they haven't known since I was a girl. My misfortune has brought them nothing but pain. I wish nothing but happiness for them.

I don't know if my eyes are opened or closed. I don't see darkness, only light. In the distance I hear voices. Ma's, I think. She sounds so worried. Why is she so worried when I am so happy?

"Maeve! Maeve!" Ma's scream is filled with horror. No, not horror...terror.

I try to tell her that I am fine, that I see the white light and it is beautiful. I try to tell her that I am walking toward the light and with each step it's getting brighter.

"Stay with me! Stay with me!" she keeps yelling. I can't see her but I can hear her as if she is standing right next to me.

I try to tell her that I am happy and to let me be, let me go. I was never good at being a human. Only bad things happened to me. I hope I make a much better angel. If I get to chose I want to watch after the twins. I try to tell her, but she won't listen. She keeps insisting that I am not going anywhere. How does she know? I am almost to the light.

Closer.

Closer.

So close now, all I can see is light and feel the heat as it engulfs me. It is warm and comforting, promising me that eternal peace will be mine in only a moment. I can't wait. Then it is gone. No warning, nothing but darkness.

I am cold.

So cold.

It is dark and there is nothing but emptiness and silence. Then in the distance I hear beeping, a constant beeping.

Where am I?

The weightlessness is gone.

I'm no longer floating anymore.

I feel every part of my body.

I open my eyes and all I want to do is close them, seal them shut forever.

They saved me.

They went against my wishes and brought me back. I am Maeve O'Malley again, just *FECKING* great. What about what I wanted? Don't I get a say? I glance around the *hospital room*. There are flowers and balloons everywhere. My ma and da are sitting in chairs on each side of me. Well, they are sleeping. There is another person in a chair in the farthest corner of the room—Miles.

I decide not to speak and pretend to be asleep. The longer I pretend the longer I can avoid the life I worked so hard to escape. There is a soft knock on my room door. Followed by shoes against the floor.

"Dr. Peterson," Da says.

"Mr. and Mrs. O'Malley. We have good news. Maeve will be just fine. Well, physically."

I hear a collective exhalation of breaths held too long.

"If she is fine then why won't she wake up?" Ma's voice sounds strained.

I feel awful for putting them through this, especially after being gone for a year. But I know the second they release me and I get the chance I will do it again. I don't want to be here anymore.

"Give her some time. She's a strong lass, but she has been through a lot. I don't want to push things on you all at once, so I will speak with all of you when she wakes up. Your daughter needs a lot of help to get through what she has suffered."

"Yes. We know that now," Da says.

"I just want her to wake, I need to hear her voice," Ma says and I hear the sobs escape her.

I know if I would open my eyes she could have the relief she craves but I am not ready for her to tell me how happy she is that I am okay and alive when I am not any of those things. Next time I will make sure I am not home and my method is quick and not survivable.

"I'll leave you, then," the doctor says.

"We'll walk you out. Miles, keep an eye and call us if she so much as stirs. I'm gonna take her ma to get a cup of tea."

"Yes, sir."

It is quiet when I open one eye and then the next. Miles is right next to me, occupying one of the chairs my folks were sitting in. He isn't surprised that my eyes are open.

"I knew you were awake," he says. He takes one of my hands into his.

"How?"

"The way you were breathing," he says.

He leans forward and regards me for the longest time in silence. "I'm so worried about you, Maeve."

"I'm worried about me too."

"I get why you aren't ready to face your folks...but you need to talk to me."

"I was happy to come home. Really, I was. When I was released that was all I wanted..." I can't help the tears that begin to fall. "To be here." I am not ashamed of what I attempted. I find his eyes and I gaze into them. He is patient. "But it isn't what I hoped it would be. Not just with Keegan, but my folks too. They expect me to be happy old Maeve and I don't really know who that is anymore. The bottom line is that I am not happy, Miles, I'm miserable. The whole time my folks were talking with the doctor, I kept thinking over and over that I am going to try and off myself the second I get out of here. Am I crazy?"

Miles leans in closer to me and takes both my hands into his. His hand is warm and strong, enveloping both of mine. We haven't known each other long but I can feel his concern for me and it is genuine. "No, you are not crazy. You're afraid. But I can't let you do that. I won't let that happen."

More tears roll out. I take one of my hands away and wipe my running nose with the back of my hand. Miles takes it back, snot and all. "Why? What is so important on this earth that I need to stick around for? Why do you even care?" I say, staring into his eyes.

Miles brings my hands to his face and kisses each one of my fingers. Before he says anything he lets out a heavy sigh. "You deserve a chance to be happy. If you leave now, you leave behind the legacy of the unfortunate girl who only knew tragedy. Why would you want that to be what people remember about you? You want to leave your family haunted with those kind of memories?"

I shake my head no. I don't want that for my family.

"Shit, Maeve, don't you want to fight back and win?"

What does he mean? If I had any fight in me I wouldn't be in this bed. "How? How can I win when my life is shite? Around every corner is a reminder of all that I have lost. I am fearful of my own shadow, Miles. I'm so tired of being me!"

Miles moves onto the edge of my bed. "Then do something about it."

"I tried."

"Not this."

"What then?"

"If you are so miserable here then leave. The world is huge. Maybe you need a change of scenery."

We are silent for the longest time. Maybe he is right. I never stood a chance here.

"I think I have an idea," I say.

"I'm listening."

"You would most likely lose your job, but you would have my undying gratitude."

He leans in closer.

"I am not going to kill you, Maeve. Nor am I going to help you do it. So don't even ask that bullshit. If god wanted you dead, you wouldn't be here right now."

I take a few deep breaths. "Take me away from here. We could go to America. You know I have citizenship there. You said it yourself—the world is huge. I won't just disappear. I will let my folks know I'm okay. I just, I can't be here around all of them and my crazy ex-fiancé. I can't get better under these conditions. And the doctor, I know what he plans to do—give me mind-numbing drugs. Which sound promising on one hand, but on another, now that I have this idea, I think you could help me. Away from here. And you would still be protecting me, still doing your job."

Miles sits back in the chair, a surefire sign that he is rejecting my plan. He stares into my eyes, searching, for what I don't know. "If I do this, Maeve, you can't be trying to kill yourself. You have to trust me to keep you safe and get better. We would not have more than a business relationship, a friendship, because I think anything more would not be helpful to you at all."

I sit up in my hospital bed. My head spins. "How long have I been out?" I ask, holding onto my head, hoping to slow down the spinning.

"Three days."

"Geesh. Okay, I agree, and Miles, thank you so much. I owe you big. I will pay for all of our expenses."

"Rest now. We can figure it all out. You need to play the role to get your folks not to send you to a lockup psychiatric facility." He takes out his phone and dials a number. After a few rings he begins speaking. "Mr. O'Malley, sir, your daughter is awake."

Only minutes go by before my folks noisily make their way into my room. I mean, I can hear them before they even enter.

"Dear Lord, Maeve!" Ma says. "What have you done!" She cries.

"Melanie, please don't make her feel worse. This is our fault. We should have made sure she was okay. I tell you one thing, that Keegan will never show his face around you or speak ill of you again. I beat him sideways, and I beat his pa too for trying to help him!"

"Da! Really? I wish I was there to see that. He deserved all of it." That bit of news put a smile on my face. "I'm really sorry about what I did. I don't even know why I did it. I have just been through so much. I know I need help."

They both wrap me in a group hug, the kind my family is notorious for. "We will get through this together, love," Ma says.

9

MILES: SAVIOR IN DISGUISE

I don't know what my draw to this girl is, unless I've turned into the cliché "savior of the damsel in distress" dude. But that can't be true, because if I was that guy I would have fallen for so many in the past, as a teen, even as a young boy. The savior gene starts early and I never had it. I mean, sure I protected my friends and family growing up, but I never fell for the girl because she needed saving. On the contrary, I have always been attracted to the woman who was confident in herself and brave. Maybe I see that in Maeve even though she doesn't. She is so much stronger than she thinks, even with the shitty hand she has been dealt.

But this—suicide. Why, because of some shit-for-brains asshole who doesn't deserve her? These are dangerous waters and I'm getting in way over my head. But hell, I already said yes, because I do believe there is a strength in her that never had a chance to develop, causing her to live in fear.

What would my father say? I know what he'd say. He'd say I've lost my fucking mind if I think it is okay to take her away from here. That this is not the job I signed up for. But then, he didn't look into her eyes and see the fear and the pain. All I want to do is take that away from her.

No more pain for Maeve. For some reason she has put that faith and hope in me, and I think if we can keep things platonic between us we may have success. She is fucking beautiful and full of life. I can see that without the fear and pain she would twinkle and sparkle like a star in the sky.

Helping her is a gift.

To make her whole again is my new life's mission. She deserves the chance to live the rest of her life without fear. She deserves to walk with her head held high, no matter who she comes in contact with from her past. More important, she needs to know how to make a motherfucker pay in blood for any ill-will he intends her. I will make sure that happens.

It doesn't matter that I have so obviously turned into the savior and fallen for the damsel, because I can't help but love her. *Damn.* If something grows from this in the future, it'll be interesting to see how her father would take to his daughter falling for a black man.

Now that Maeve and I have a plan. I need to set things in motion. Working in security I have friends everywhere. I need their discretion though, because if my dad catches wind of my plan, that's my ass.

I decide on Vegas as the city of choice, because it is easy to get lost in that crowd. I put in a call to my friends at a local gun range. I put in my order for weapons. Two Glock 22s, a Beretta 93R, and a Glock 43 for Maeve. Also, an array of my favorite knives.

The last piece of the puzzle is sneaking away from Dublin with the girl who considers herself the unluckiest girl in the world, and whisking her off to America. I know I have lost my damn mind.

10

MAEVE: TIME TO HEAL

*I*t takes a full week before I get to come home from the hospital and a complete psychiatric workup. I passed enough that I don't have to be locked down, but I have a schedule of appointments with my new psychiatrist, group grief counseling, and a prescription for anti-depressants. All of which I'm sure would work for me, and even help me get better, but they are not on my menu.

I am surprised that they are trusting me enough to let me sleep alone in my room tonight. But Ma will no doubt check on me all night, which will make slipping out a challenge.

Miles has already secured tickets out of Ireland for tonight after everyone is asleep, including my guards. I am not a child. I am leaving of my own free will. So while my folks will worry, it won't be like the second time or the first.

Thankfully, I have four million dollars which means I won't have to call upon my folks for aid during my recovery. For the second time in a very short time, I write a note to my family.

I'M OKAY.

I am not going to harm myself. I am leaving to find myself. Please do not blame Miles. He came with me so I wouldn't be alone because I know Da wants me to have protection. I was going to leave with him or without him, and, knowing that, he chose to accompany me so that you would know I would be safe. Please don't come to get me. I promise I will be home when I am well enough and strong enough to stand on my own two feet. I will keep in regular touch with you.

Love,

Maeve

WHEN THE HOUSE is sufficiently quiet, I make my way to our meeting point, only a two-minute walk outside my family's property. I don't bring anything with me beyond what will fit into my medium-sized handbag.

The air outside is cool and wet—May in Dublin. I can't explain the reason, but the closer I get to our meeting spot, the higher I can hold my head up. The freer I feel. This is exactly what I need.

The taillights glow bright through the foggy night and I can hear the low hum of the engine.

My escape.

I open the passenger door and climb in. Miles offers me a nervous smile. I ask so much of him for doing this for me because I am costing him his entire career in the protection business. He will be known as the man who ran off with the girl he was assigned to protect. It won't matter that I asked him to accompany me. It won't matter that I am an adult, because that is not the job he signed on for. I am not his employer, my da is, and in this case proper protocol would be for him to report my intentions to my da. I will have to figure out a way to thank him. Perhaps a large portion of the money Mason gave me. At least he wouldn't have to worry about employment for a long time. Who am I kidding? In this economy, at least for a little while.

"Are you sure about this, Miles?"

He doesn't blink when he gazes at me. "Yes, I am very sure. You?"

I nod.

We pull out onto the small road and I don't look back. The airport is about an hour's drive from my home. The car is thick with nerves and fear because we are not in the clear until we board that plane. And even then, we are not clear until we land on U.S. soil. My folks are going to have a hard time with my decision, but I hope they understand.

WE MAKE it through security without a hitch. I feel like I am in an action movie.

Miles and I are on the lam. I am a material witness and he is trying to get me into the U.S. before we are captured by the bad guys.

My pulse is racing while we sit on the plane. Still, I have not spoken, because at every step of our journey I have expected my folks to come busting in to stop me from leaving. It is only when our plane begins taxiing on the runway that I begin to allow myself to calm. When we are airborne, I breathe, letting out the deep breath my body wouldn't allow me to release before.

Miles reaches over and squeezes my hand. When I look into his eyes I see that he is more relaxed. Who knows what would have happened to him if we were intercepted before leaving.

"Thank you," I say to Miles, my hand still in his. "Is it strange that I feel better already? I mean, it doesn't hurt so much to breathe."

"Don't think of it, Maeve. You deserve a fresh start. You can always return home when you are ready."

I squeeze his hand. He has no idea the gift he has given me, asking nothing of me in return. I am so lucky to have him in my life. Wow, that was the first time I have ever considered myself lucky. "Where are we headed?" I ask when I realize that I was in such a hurry to get out of Dublin I never found out our destination. Not that it matters. Anywhere will do.

"Las Vegas. I figured it's touristy and thousands move there every month. We will blend right in."

The idea of that makes me smile. No exes lurking around every corner, accusing me of stalking them. No unknowing, long-lost friends asking the dreaded questions. No family members hovering over me with worry, and no three-man security team following me everywhere I go. I mean, sure Miles will be with me and I am sure my safety is of the upmost importance to him, but somehow these terms seem closer to my own.

"I have a friend in Las Vegas. Her name is Vivian. She was there with me."

"You should connect with her. It's good for you to spend some time with someone who understands what you went through."

I nod.

The farther we travel away from my home, the more possibilities I can envision in my life. The idea that I only have to worry about me is wonderful. I fall into a dreamless sleep as we coast toward my new future.

11

MAEVE: VIVA LAS VEGAS

*W*e touch down at McCarran Airport in the middle of the day. I can feel the Vegas May heat when we hit the tarmac. It is an arid heat, so different from the moisture of home. *Yes.*

Without checked bags Miles and I head to the curb for a cab. I have heard of the casino-like atmosphere in the airport here, but never seen slot machines up close and personal before.

"MGM, please," Miles instructs the driver.

The smile on my face must be infectious because Miles is sharing it. He really has turned out to be a great friend, saving me. It takes minutes to get to the MGM.

"We're here!" I shout when we exit the cab. I wrap Miles up in a squealy hug. His arms fold around mine. My excitement gives way to something deeper: utter gratitude and appreciation. We stand at the entrance with our arms around each other. To any onlooker, we are a couple who are probably coming to Vegas to tie the knot. The reality is that Miles is my savior and I owe him everything for giving up so much for me. "Thank you," I say again but this time in his ear.

"You are so welcome. Let's go get checked in," he says, taking me by the hand.

There is an open checker-inner person, so we walk right up. I speak before Miles can. I want to splurge on him in thanks. "We will be needing an extended stay in your finest accommodations," I say. I steal a look at Miles and offer him a smile. He knows that he isn't going to win here.

"How long do you plan on staying with us, ma'am?" the man asks.

Ma'am? I'm only twenty-two. "At least a month. Right, love?" I check with Miles.

He nods. "A month, possibly two. A two-bedroom suite." He holds up two fingers.

"You heard the man," I say. I couldn't hide my excitement if I tried.

The man nods. "We have just the thing in our Signature suites. Strip view, very upscale and comfortable. Just need a credit card and photo ID. I will have to charge the first fifteen days of your stay."

I hand the man my Chamber bankcard. "Not a problem." The man hands me back my card and busies himself gathering things for us. "Oh, and, please do not send calls to our room. We will come down and check for messages."

"Understood."

We are given keys to our suite, the spa and the pool, along with VIP passes for this or that.

"Enjoy your stay with us," he calls after us.

"Ready?" Miles asks me.

"Very."

We thank the gentleman for his assistance before making our way toward the suites, hand in hand.

OUR ROOM IS GORGEOUS. The view of the Strip is amazing. I bet when the sun goes down we will feel like we are in the middle of Las Vegas's *craic*. I feel it—I know I can be anyone here. Not Maeve the ex-kidnapping victim, twice. Not ex-Chambermaid. And most important, no one will ever walk up to me here and say, "Hey Maeve, when are you getting married?" or "I heard what happened to you and

Keegan." I won't have to see his evil face forever if I want. This was the best decision I could have ever made.

"So, I am going to take the room closest to the entry door. Any intruder will have to pass by me to get to you."

I am too busy dancing around the room with joy to care where he sleeps. Or myself, for that matter. "Sounds wonderful, love."

"Come here, Maeve."

I skip to him and he wraps me into another surprising hug. "You do not know how good it makes me to feel that you are happy. I think this was an excellent decision."

I squeeze him tight. "I agree. Let's go eat! And buy some clothes! Oh please tell me you like sushi?" I ask.

"Love it."

Miles and I make our way like any other excited tourists toward the nearest sushi spot in the hotel. I am starving. When we are seated I order salt and pepper calamari, potstickers, and lettuce wraps. When the waitress puts them in front of us I pick up my chopsticks and go to town.

"Sorry, I think I might physically be dying of hunger right now. I hijacked the appetizers," I say and giggle.

"I'm good. I am happy to see you eating," he says and follows it up with the most amazing smile that travels all the way up to his eyes. His face is everything.

He doesn't even pick up his chopsticks, he just watches me eat. I would have had to fight Keegan for a share of food.

When the waitress returns with cucumber salads, I also order a couple of Sapporos. "Please have one beer with me."

"Nope."

"Come on, you can't always be on. Hell, I'll drink them both. I'm not driving."

Miles laughs at me and leans back in his seat and watches me. "I will have a *couple* of beers with you, Maeve."

"Yay," I say. I dig into my salad. *Mmm, so good.* "So you must have a hard time keeping a girlfriend in your line of work?" I inquire between bites.

He picks up his chopsticks and begins eating. He doesn't look up when he answers me. "The traveling makes it nearly impossible," he says, and finally looks up at me.

I can only imagine. "Are you planning to do this career forever? I mean, you are an amazing man. Wouldn't be fair to keep yourself single and deprive a nice young woman of your company." I flirt. I can't help myself around him. Miles is beauty, sex, and chivalry wrapped into six foot two, one hundred and eighty-five pounds of fecking wonderful.

"You have any nice young woman in mind?"

Oh, he flirts back. "I may know a nice young gal. She has some healing to do, but if you don't mind a little damaged package..."

Miles's playful smile evaporates and he sits up straight in his seat. "Stop, Maeve. You are no more damaged than anyone else on this planet. Sure, you've been through some shit, but you have to start seeing yourself as more than the shit you've been through. No man, and I mean no man worth anything is going to want to be with you."

I blanch.

"Let me finish. Not because of what you've been through, Maeve, but because of how you see yourself. A man isn't going to treat a woman who loves herself like shit. You know why?"

It must be a rhetorical question because he doesn't give me the chance to answer.

"He won't treat that woman like shit because she won't let him. Why do you think you were willing to be with Keegan? Why you still wanted him after he dumped you? Maeve, you have to fall in love with Maeve first and I promise you will be fighting off some pretty awesome fucking guys. I know I would be in that line," he says and relaxes back into his seat and takes a long draw of his beer, his eyes not leaving mine.

I almost leap over the table to put my lips to his. "Well, damn. I can't argue with that, and I get it." I pause to take a sip of my beer. He is absolutely right. I would have taken Keegan back without a thought. I don't see myself the way I should, but after everything I have been through, I don't know how. But I am willing to try. "I am a work in progress. But when I finish my little self-improvement project, your ass better be in that line," I say, not able to hide my smile.

"I'm so glad I met you," Miles says.

I raise my glass, he raises his, and we tap them against one another.

The waiter interrupts us, placing more appetizers in front of us on the table. "You can order the rolls," I say to Miles.

"Thanks, madame," he teases. "Bring us your six most popular rolls, and two more Sapporos," Miles says, smiling and obviously proud of himself. "I'm going to excuse myself to the restroom. Are you going to be okay?"

"Of course. What could happen to me here?"

Miles's eyebrow raising into his scalp tells me he thinks differently.

～

WHEN HE RETURNS, our main dishes start showing up and it looks more like a table of food for five or six, not two.

There isn't much conversation now that the food is in front of us. We devour all of it. All of it. "I don't think we have to worry about walking back to the room because we should be able to swim there," I say.

Miles laughs at my joke. Wow. Where did he come from? I mean, with Keegan, I felt like I had to be on all of the time. The perfect future wife of this man who believed he was going to be important. You know, the "order a salad and be sure not to finish my food" girl. I would never ravish my food like I just did. I made all of this sushi my bitch, as one of my Chamber sisters, Sapphire, used to say. *Who am I?*

The more time I spend with Miles, the more I realize I was not truly myself with Keegan. I was being the woman he wanted me to be. Miles wants me to find myself and fall in love with me. Like I said, where did he come from?

"When they bring the check it's mine!" I say. "You risked so much doing this for me, so I don't want you to spend a dime as long as we are here," I continue.

"Understood."

I sit back in my seat, completely satisfied. Miles does the same. I could see myself loving him. In fact, I think part of me already does. How could I not? I don't know how much we have in common yet, besides loving sushi, but he is so easy to talk to.

The waiter comes with the check and sets it in front of Miles. They always assume the man is going to pay.

"Your receipt, sir," the waiter says. "Your tip was most gracious," he adds.

My mouth flies open and Miles can't help but laugh. "Sneaky, very sneaky," I say.

"You are welcome. Let's go get some clothes."

"Thank you, and you may have to roll me. Can we sleep instead of shop?"

"We sure can."

We make our way to our room and I fall into my bed, clothes and all.

12

MILES: SACRIFICES

*M*aeve is out the second she climbs into bed. She asked me to keep the door ajar. It makes me feel awful that she is so afraid, and it makes me feel special that she really trusts me. I have to make sure that I am always deserving of that trust.

I plop down on the sofa, my stomach bloated from our sushi gorge-fest. I never knew a girl so small could eat so much. Maeve is forever surprising me. All I want for her is her complete happiness.

My phone vibrates on the table and when I flip it over my stomach drops when I see my father's number flash across the screen. *Shit!*

"Hey, Pops," I say into the receiver. I was waiting for this phone call.

"Have you lost your damn mind? You can't go running off with your assignment, Miles! Peter O'Malley called me and said you disappeared with his pride and joy! What the hell would possess you to risk your entire career for this girl?"

"I love her." *Shit. I can't believe I just copped to that.*

"You *have* lost your damn mind! Where are you? I'm coming to get *you* and take *her* back to Dublin!"

"The fuck you are! She needs this. Her parents were smothering her and her ex-fiancé was abusive. She can't get better there. She is an adult. She asked me for help and I am helping her. End of story." I dare say bold and explosive words to my father in a way that I have never uttered.

"Then you can kiss your career goodbye." He slams the phone down in my face.

He is probably right. My career in protection is going to be over when rumors travel through our circuit that I ran off with the daughter of the man who hired me. But I can't worry about that right now. Sometimes when you are helping someone you have to leap with them and hope things will turn out okay.

My phone vibrates again.

"Yep?" I say into the receiver. I knew my pops would call back. He would never end our conversation on such a bad note. That is not his style.

"Are you sure about this, son?"

"Yes I am very sure. You should see her, Pops. The farther she got from Dublin, the deeper she could breathe. She is coming to life."

"But ask yourself what happens when she goes back. She can't run from her problems, son. How is this helping her?"

I flop onto the sofa. "We are not running. Her problem is that her father never taught her to take care of herself. I get it. He thought he would be enough to keep her safe. But that wasn't the case. She was kidnapped twice. Who gets kidnapped twice and manages to return back to their old life and just jumps back in? I'm going to train her to defend herself, to stop being a victim, to see with special eyes, head-on-a-swivel-type shit, Pops. Then when she goes back she will feel empowered to meet her life head-on. I'm not expecting her to chose me when she is ready to go home either, 'cause love isn't selfish like that. I want her happy and strong. That's all."

There is silence. I am waiting for the shouting to begin. "Then, son, I am proud of you. If you need anything at all you let me know."

"Wow, thanks." I pull my phone from my ear and look at it. Am I hallucinating? "Really? Why?" I have to know why he would feel this way when I have so obviously gone against every rule in the book.

"Because I know your heart, son. You didn't choose this path because it is easy. You chose it because you believed it was the right thing to do. You saw someone who needed our help and you are giving it to her, no matter the cost. How can I not be proud? I will speak with Peter O'Malley on this matter."

"Thanks, Pops."

We hang up on a shocking note. I never expected my dad to agree with my decision, but I am happy to have him on my side.

13

MAEVE: DREAMS AND NIGHTMARES

I am out without a thought, but this time I dream.

Miles has just punched Keegan in the face. I run up to him and jump into his arms in thanks for beating up Keegan. Miles attempts to set me down but I won't let him. I want to be in his arms forever. When our faces are only inches apart I take my opportunity and kiss him. He doesn't resist. Instead his tongue slips into my mouth and I am a ball of sexual need and want. It is oozing from every pore and my panties are wet with antici-pation. "I want you."

Miles walks me into what would be my room, except it looks nothing like my room. It is shimmery jade green with gold accent furniture. We are completely naked and it feels right.

"What's this?" Miles asks, pointing at my pleasure pony. "It looks like it should be on a carousel but this is no kids' play toy."

"I'll show you." I walk over to my armoire and grab a healthy-sized dildo. His eyebrow raises in curiosity. I cross the room and screw it onto the pony's back. I push the button and we watch it glisten as lubricant covers and drips down the shaft. I dare a look down and he too is ready. His meaty cock is ready for action.

Before I show him the full workings of the pony, I want to thank him more. I ease down onto my knees and take him into my hand. The skin is a smooth, warm covering over steel. I wrap my lips around him and thank the tip with my tongue swirling round and round. Then I take him deep into my mouth, until I can feel him at the back of my throat. Then I suck him. He pulls out of my mouth and looks at me with shock and awe.

"Join me," I say. I climb onto the pony facing backward. He climbs on with me, watching me with lustful eyes as I sink down on the long shaft, letting a moan escape from the back of my throat. Miles's eyes grow big and then small as he enjoys my self-pleasure. Not content with being a spectator, he finds my nipple with his lips and his sucking makes me want to scream. I almost come undone when his other hand cups my clitoris and his fingers begin working on my pleasure nugget. I combust grinding on my oversized dildo, with Miles devouring my breasts and tantalizing my clit. Feck yeah.

When I open my eyes I wish I hadn't because we are not alone.

"My turn with the little whore," Keegan says, his cock swinging in wait. He snatches me off the pony. I look around for Miles and he is gone. The only people in the room with me are a naked and very erect Keegan and Mason.

The screams that escape me wake me from my sleep.

"Maeve! Maeve!"

"Miles! Oh my goodness. Miles, don't leave me again!"

His arms comfort me, enveloping me with concern and care. I sob heavily into them. "You're safe. I'm here. I won't go anywhere. Try and sleep." I lie back down and Miles lies next to me, his arms around me.

"My dream started out so beautiful, perfect, and then nothing but darkness. It was so scary." I sniff.

"I'm sorry. I wish I could reach in and take all the bad dreams and memories out of your head." He squeezes me tighter.

"This helps." I tighten my grip on his arms, instantly feeling less afraid of what will happen when I close my eyes.

14

MAEVE: RESTFUL NIGHT

When I wake up I feel refreshed. I am still in Miles's arms and he is silent behind me. I have no idea what time it is. Midday naps are the worst because I am always disoriented. I begin to move and Miles's arms tighten around me.

"Where are you getting off to?" he asks, immediately releasing me.

"Bathroom."

"I call next," he says.

"Uh, look around, I think this place has three bathrooms." I wave my hands for effect.

"True," he says and hops up.

I move quick as we race to the closest bathroom. I win, I'm sure because he let me. When I make it to the living room area, the curtains are drawn and the view is every bit as amazing as I expected.

"How'd you sleep?"

"Like a dreamless log. Thank you for sleeping with me. Can that be a thing for a while? I mean, I hate to ask you to blur the lines of our friendship like this, but I am terrified to go to sleep."

He crosses the room to me and wraps me in a hug that melts me.

"Well, as your protector and friend I can't have you terrified, so consider it done."

"Thank you, Miles. I don't know what I would do without you."

A small laugh escapes him. "Well, I will see how you feel about that when we talk about some of the activities you will be participating in while we are here." He takes a seat in a chair that overlooks the view of the Strip out of the gargantuan window.

I follow and take a seat across from him. "I'm listening."

"Okay, so for starters I think part of your fear is a feeling of helplessness. Your parents hired us because they too believe that you are helpless, but you don't have to be. Starting tomorrow, you and I will be training. Shooting, fighting, and observation lessons."

I pout a little. "That doesn't sound like much Vegas fun."

He grabs my knees and gives them a squeeze. "Oh, we will have that too. We can even reach out to your friend Vivian and see if she and her boyfriend want to do some couple stuff," he says.

"You said couple stuff. Are we a couple?" *Please say yes. Please say yes.*

"No. As much as I would love to be a couple with you, Maeve, that isn't what you need right now. You need me to be your friend. You need me to teach you to be so strong that no one can hurt you again. It breaks my heart to see you so broken and I wanted to put a toe tag on the douche back in Ireland. But this is the only way I can see to help you."

I pout, then smile. "Well, that makes me want you less. Shite, did I say that out loud?" I cover my mouth.

Miles's laugh is hearty and I think he may have just blushed. "Behave yourself. Besides, when I tell you the next thing you have to do, you won't want me at all." He hands me a cell phone, like an olden days flippy phone.

"What's this for?"

"Call your folks. The phone is clean. They can't call you back on it."

"Miles, it's like two a.m. in Dublin!"

"If you were a parent would that time matter to you?"

I sulk. "I guess not." I mouth *I hate you* to him as I dial home.

He laughs again. "I knew that you would."

Of course someone picks up on the first ring. "*Anseo*?" My da's voice is sleepy but alert. Only bad calls happen in the middle of the night/morning.

"It's me, Da."

"Maeve! Where the hell are you? Are you okay, love? Where is Miles? Is he with you? 'Cause if he is, he is a dead man for taking you away from us."

"Is that my daughter?" I hear Ma in the background.

"Yes, love, it's her," he whispers.

"Did you not get my letter? Miles didn't take me anywhere. I confided in him that I was leaving and I asked him to travel with me so that I am not alone. I trust him with my life, Da. He is going to train me on how to protect myself."

Ma snatches the phone. "You get on the first plane back here, young lady. You hear what I'm tellin' you?"

I hold the phone in my hand away from my ear, while they fight over who is going to talk to me. I look up to heaven and then to Miles for strength before I put the phone to my ear. "Listen, you two. I am not coming home until I am good and damned ready. I am an adult, or have you both forgotten that? I am not strong enough to be there right now. It is too painful yet. I will return home and when I do I will be a new and improved, stronger Maeve. Miles is going to help me with that. He is a good friend. Now, I am going to put the speaker on and the two of you are going to thank him for taking all of this on when he didn't have to." I push the speaker button. "Talk," I order.

"Miles, the wife and I want to thank you for taking care of our Maeve. We know she is in good hands."

I can tell that was difficult for my da. But I can't have them blaming Miles for just being an awesome guy. "Better. I will call you in a few days to check in. I love you both," I say. "Kiss the twins for me."

"We love you too, baby girl. Be safe, and we will be seeing you soon?"

"Yes, Da, as soon as I am ready."

We say our goodbyes and I disconnect the call.

"I knew you had some strength in there," Miles says.

"Doesn't count when they're my folks."

"It's a start. You hungry?"

"Famished," I say.

"How a little tiny thing like you can eat so much is a mystery to me."

We decide on room service. Cheese pizza. Another thing we have in common. Miles runs down to the store inside the hotel and brings back some beer options. Sapporo, Guinness, and Blue Moon. A beer party. We sit on the floor in the living room drinking beer, eating pizza, and watching pay per view movies—comedies.

We decide to hide the beers under the ice, in the ice chest that he bought, and whichever one we pull out we have to drink. Since I only like one out of the three, this is a challenge, and the absolute most fun I have had with a man in as long as I can remember. Just innocent fun.

"You asked me if I wanted to be in security forever."

"I did, and you never gave me an answer," I say.

"Well, the answer is no. I consider the time I have spent and am spending as on-the-job training for my ultimate career."

"You don't need all of this training to be my husband. Trust me, I'm not that much work!" I tease, the beer making me silly and brave.

"Ha ha. Actually, *you* are a lot of work," he teases back. "I was saying before I was interrupted."

I stick my tongue out at him and he copies me.

"I want to run a training center. With defense classes for children, women, the elderly. I also want an academy that produces the finest high-level security agents in the world. That will allow me to settle down and have a wonderful life with a vibrant and beautiful woman who loves sushi and cheese pizza as much as I do."

I roll my eyes. "Ha ha, I got the joke. But seriously, that is an amazing plan. You get everything you want in life with a plan like that."

"Precisely."

"Well you, sir, deserve all of your dreams to come true and more."

"As do you, my lady."

What he says hits me and sadness clouds over me. I don't want to spoil our good time but I realize I have no idea what my dreams are anymore.

"You can always create new dreams, Maeve," Miles says, reading my mind.

"Am I that easy to read?" I ask, my face a mask of shock.

"Transparent."

"Well I will drink to that. But then I'm Irish, so I will kind of drink to anything," I tease.

Miles is right, though. It is time I create new dreams for myself. Who says that the path I was on was the right one? Maybe being kidnapped had to happen so that I wouldn't end up as an unhappy trophy wife. Also, if it hadn't happened I would have never met Miles, and every moment I spend with him tells me that meeting him is a gift.

15

MILES: SECOND SIGHT

I plan to take it easy on Maeve today, but training starts now. At the end of our training session her surprise will arrive. Maybe that is how we can arrange this: work, followed by reward. Incentive is always more motivating. I slide out of the bed so I don't wake her. She is a hard sleeper, I have noticed.

I turn toward the bed when I shouldn't. Keeping our relationship platonic has been a challenge, because Maeve is fucking amazing! Adding sleeping together every night is definitely a judgment-clouder, but if it helps her escape the nightmares I will continue to do it without thought.

She is so beautiful. Soft, creamy skin dusted with a healthy share of freckles. Red hair flowing over her pillow and down her back. Her body is equally beautiful—swimsuit model, this—with just the right amount of curves. Delicate. Everything about Maeve O'Malley is delicate. How can anyone hurt her? Keeping her safe is my first priority and helping her become a fighter is my second. Falling in love with her is one of those unforeseen challenges of the job. It is not unseen or unheard of. I'm sure it happens more than I know, but I can't let my emotions guide my actions. Maeve can't afford for me to.

After a couple of deep breaths I walk out of the room of this woman who trusts me with her life. I grab a bottled water and bypass the gym, and run through a workout in the living room area. No weights needed.

Twenty minutes later, I wake Maeve up so that she can get ready. "Hey, sleepyhead. Time to rise and shine."

She lifts her head up and stares at me like I've grown a second head. "What time is it?"

"Eight o'clock," I say, peeling my wet shirt off me.

I don't miss how her eyes widen at the sight of my exposed upper body. "In the morning? Are you insane? You get me drunk and then make me wake up at the crack of dawn?"

I can't help but laugh. "First of all, you missed the crack of dawn about three hours ago. And second, that is exactly what I'm doing. I'm heading into the other bathroom to shower. We need to get clothes today and you are starting your training immediately." I walk out of the room because her open mouth suggests a protest against everything I have said to her.

"Training? I haven't even had my tea yet!" she yells after me. The light, lyrical lilt of her voice warms my heart.

"You can have your tea while you train, Princess."

FORTY MINUTES later and Maeve and I head down to the buffet to eat. I figure that is a perfect spot for our first lesson. We don't have to wait in line because our room affords us VIP entrance. When we are seated at our table, a waitress takes our drink order. When she walks away I ask the first question.

"What color was our waitress's hair?"

Maeve looks at me as if I am insane. "I don't know? How would I know that? She was only at our table for a second."

I sit back and watch her for a few minutes. "She had blonde hair with gray streaks. She was wearing small gold hoop earrings, and a gold watch on her right hand, suggesting that she is left-handed. She was no more than five-three, but I'm sitting so I may be off by an inch one way or the other, and she limped, suggesting left hip pain. Her nails are polished with a coat of clear."

Disbelief is the look she gives me. When the waitress returns with our drinks Maeve assesses her for the first time and takes inventory of everything that I said.

"Wow, how did you do that?"

"The same way you will learn to. We get so wrapped up in what is happening in our life right in front of us, we forget to see what is going on around us. That is dangerous. Chances are if you knew how to see with your second pair of eyes, you would have noticed that you were being watched before you were taken. Before we begin defensive training, we will start here. And there's no more perfect place than Vegas's busy locale. When you are done for the day, I have a surprise for you for all the hard work."

"Yay. I love surprises."

16

MAEVE: I LOVE SURPRISES

*A*fter hours of watching people, my head hurts. I have never studied the world around me in such detail. From how many kids the lady behind us has to who's wearing glasses, hats, how tall this person is or isn't, or my best estimation of how many people are in the room with us.

Miles guides me into a coffee shop. An iced coffee is exactly what I need for my pounding headache.

"That wasn't bad for your first time," Miles compliments.

"Thanks." My iced mocha feels divine going down. "I thought my eyeballs were going to fall out, to be honest with you," I admit.

He flashes me a breathtaking smile.

We sit in amicable silence enjoying our coffee and sweets.

I find myself taking in my surroundings without being prompted to do so. My eyes take in the coffee workers—three of them, all female, busying themselves with creating tasty drinks. My eyes find the gathering line that wasn't there when we got here. I trail the line, taking in people's attributes along the way. I may as well continue my training. My eyes find a familiar couple holding hands. The woman thin with dark hair nearing her waist, the man tall, tanned, and very muscled. My eyes travel to the next person in line and then immediately back to them.

Oh my heavens, Vivian and Tyson?

My eyes shoot to Miles, who is grinning like an idiot. "Surprise!" he says.

I am out of my seat and rushing over to them. "Guys!"

They turn to greet me, not surprised at all, happy but not shocked.

"Maeve!" Vivian shouts and we wrap each other in a huge three-person embrace.

I turn back to Miles, who looks very proud of himself. "This is the best surprise ever!"

I wait with them while they get their drinks and lead them to our table. After quick introductions, I learn that Tyson's real name is Dominic.

"I can't believe you guys are here, and together! This is so perfect!"

"When Miles called us to tell us that you would be in town I couldn't wait to see you," Vivian says.

I turn to Miles. "How did you find them?"

"It's the digital age. All I needed was a name," he says and flashes me a swoon-worthy smile.

My goodness, I am falling for this guy.

My eyes sweep over my beautiful Chamber sister and her love and I am so happy for her. I wish I was in the middle of my own happily-ever-after, instead of running from angry ex-fiancés, post-suicide attempts, and a family that believes they can heal me by smothering me with love.

"So how have you been? Why are you in Vegas?" Vivian fires off questions at me.

"Long story short: Keegan turned out to be a total wanker, so that didn't work out. Uh...my family and friends can't fix me. So I ran off with my bodyguard to Vegas to see if I can fix myself. Miles is amazing."

"Maeve's da hired me and my team to watch over her back home, but being in Ireland was the worst place for this one. So here we are.

I'm gonna train her to not need any guarding, so she can take care of herself."

Dominic nods agreement. "That is a fantastic idea. I have been planning on training Vivian myself. Perhaps we can team up while you guys are in town?"

Vivian and I can't hold our composure. We squeeze hands and chant *yes*.

"I don't think we have a choice, do you?" Miles asks, looking over at us.

This is the best day of my life. Oh my goodness, not only do I get to spend all of my free time with Miles—now I get to spend time with my sister. For the second time since arriving in Las Vegas, I am considering myself lucky. Dare I hope that my luck is changing?

And just like any normal group where there are an equal number of men and women, we break off into our own conversations. The guys, planning our training. Us—well, for starters I want to know about the rock Vivian is sporting. "So?" I ask.

Vivian feigns ignorance and I point to my ring finger and give her a look that says *dish*.

"Oh, this little thing?" She waves her hand out toward me.

"Oh my goodness, Vivian, it is gorgeous! Tell me everything!"

Her smile covers her whole face. "When I got home, Dominic showed up and told me how he felt, but that he would give me the chance to chose for myself, because like you I had a guy back home before we were taken. It took about a week before I chose Dominic. He proposed and we haven't been apart since."

"So when is the big date?"

"We are thinking this summer. Why wait?"

"I am so happy for you!" I reach over to hug her. We hold the embrace forever.

"So what is going on with you and Miles? He is dreamy, Maeve," she says in a low voice, hoping that only I can hear. But knowing Miles, he has super-hearing.

I can't help but blush. I sneak a peek over at Miles. He is having a serious conversation with Dominic. He takes my safety very seriously. I'm sure Dominic feels the same about Vivian. It is too late for my friendship with Miles, as far as I am concerned. I am faking friendship because I have wanted more since the coffee shop back home. He happens to be the most amazing man I have ever known. I must have been staring too long because he turns and gazes into my eyes. There is a smile in his eyes. If I didn't know any better, based on the way he is regarding at me, I think he adores me. I blush and look away.

"You don't have to say a word. If there is one thing I know now when I see it, it's love," Vivian says.

"Oh, stop," I say, waving off her comment.

"Hey, love isn't something you plan or expect. If any couple can teach you that it's me and Dominic."

I nod. "That is very true."

"We should go out tonight, celebrate! This hotel has an amazing club," Vivian says, glancing around at us to see if we are game.

"Sounds like a good time to me," I say.

The guys agree.

I can't believe I get to party with Vivian.

WE SPENT the rest of the day shopping at the Fashion Show. Miles and I were able to purchase enough clothes to last us nearly a month before we have to do any laundry. I was excited to hit some of my favorites: Topshop, Urban Outfitters, Diesel, Victoria's Secret, and Kate Spade.

Vivian and I decide to sneak away for a bit to buy dresses for tonight. Unfortunately for us, Dominic and Miles are likeminded and we have to endure the company of Jonathan and Mitch, two of Vivian's bodyguards. These guys look the part of a couple of highly trained badasses.

Miles pulls me aside. "This is the only way that I can leave you, Maeve. I would die twice if something ever happened to you. But I trust Dominic that these guys are the best, seeing how we have similar interests in protecting our girls."

S w o o n i n g. My tongue feels numb with my desire to kiss him. Am I his girl? Is that how he sees me? I certainly hope so.

The guys decide to head back to the hotel, taking our purchases with them. I was so happy because I was tiring of carrying so much, and I only had a few of the bags.

"Sorry, Dominic won't let me out of his sight...or theirs," Vivian says and points in the direction of our new friends.

"It's okay. He obviously loves you very much. After what we've been through I guess one can never be too cautious."

Vivian gives Dominic a quick peck and I wave sweetly to Miles, wishing I could kiss him like that. Shite, I have it bad. Jonathan and Mitch give us a modicum of space, so that the unknowing eye wouldn't even suspect that they are with us. Vivian grabs my hand, squeezes it, but doesn't let go. Hand in hand, we take on the mall. Her gesture tells me so much: I am not alone; I can be strong; I can survive the things that *we* went through. Knowing that she went through what I went through and worse is the comfort I need. I squeeze hers in return.

17

MILES: CROSSING THE LINE

*S*eeing Maeve enjoy so many smiles is an answered prayer. She is the most beautiful woman I have ever seen. Not because of her outward appearance, though she is a stunner. But that is not it—she glows from the inside. Her light may be fractured because of her personal experiences but I have glimpsed her brightness. She has the heart and kindness of a dreamer, who sees the best in everyone. I know that when she is whole again she will shine brighter than a diamond. I witnessed it today in the presence of Vivian and Dominic. I can see her joy. It is infectious, the kind of thing that will give a man hope that anything is possible.

Everything about her makes remaining friends one of the hardest thing I have ever done. Watching her walk away hand in hand with Vivian, I must have had the dumbest smile on my face.

"Bro, you got it bad, hunh?" Dominic says as I gaze after her.

"What, no," I say, trying to cover.

"Okay, man. Whatever you say. Trust me, she feels the same way about you," he says.

I look at him, startled and hopeful. "Seriously, how do you know?"

"I'm just messing with you," Dominic says.

I shove his shoulder. "Not funny."

"No, seriously. I think the world can see it. As far as she is concerned, you hung the moon. She is crazy about you."

"Well, I hope you're right. Because I am falling hard for her."

Dominic and I take the five million shopping bags and head for the nearest cab.

"You're sure your men will keep them safe? Maybe I should head back inside," I say, because my nerves are getting the best of me. I don't feel right leaving her. The world is an important place and Maeve is my entire world.

"They are ex-special forces. Nothing and no one is going to get near them, I promise."

I grimace and nod before hopping in the cab.

WE DECIDE to make reservations at Hakkasan and a VIP booth at the Ling Ling Lounge. Tonight is going to be special for Maeve.

We stop off at the coffee shop and just kick back. "So, knowing what you know about how we feel about each other, what should I do about it?" I ask Dominic.

"You go for it, for her. Do you believe you can make her happy?"

"Happier than anyone else can."

"Then what are you waiting for? Do you know how I met Vivian?"

I shake my head.

"I worked at that place where they were taken. I was a guard there, hired to protect the women. I was in a dark place. My mother and I were gunned down like we were nothing. I survived, she didn't. When Vivian got there I was her personal guard. I'd never done that before, been a personal guard. I snapped out of my depression and realized this place was wrong. I am planning to find this place again and bring the whole organization down. That, and keeping Vivian safe, is my life's mission. But I will tell you if your love can save Maeve, then love her with everything you got, 'cause Vivian saved me.

She loved me to life. I see it, the way Maeve looks at you. She is waiting for you to take the first step."

I sit back and think about everything he just said to me. I don't believe in judging someone unless I have walked a mile in their shoes, but I know if my mother was gunned down in front of me, my world would go dark too. And you can't see shit in that darkness—right, wrong, love, hate. That kind of darkness can make you go blind.

"How can I train her to be a fighter if we are together? Won't that make doing my job harder?" I ask.

"The way I see it, the second she is yours it will no longer be your job. It'll be the most important mission of your life to keep all that is yours safe. Trust me."

"Thanks, man. I think you are right."

Maeve and Miles. Sounds good together.

18

MAEVE: ALL DRESSED UP

"This is the best day I have had since being out," Vivian says and she gives me a soft hip check.

"Me too." I check her back.

After walking in and out of a million stores, we both find our dresses at Neiman's.

"Dominic and Miles will shit twice and die when they see us in these tonight," Vivian gushes.

"Interesting expression, but I know, right?" I agree as I hand the cashier my bankcard. I can't contain the smile that overcomes my face. "Is it wrong for me to like him so much? I mean, he says we shouldn't cloud the lines of our friendship while I am healing. I feel guilty for betraying him like this."

The cashier slips my dress into a clear Neiman's garment bag instead of folding it. I smile and thank her for taking such care.

Vivian takes her turn with her purchase. "Who says he isn't how you are supposed to heal yourself? I never imagined Dominic coming into my life, and I could never be happier. Maybe he is your HEA," she says, taking her proffered dress on its hanger.

"What does that mean?" I ask as we walk through the store with our gorgeous dresses in hand.

"Happily ever after." She turns toward me, stopping us in the middle of the store. "You survived The Chamber. We all did. You might not have gone in there strong, but anyone who comes out of there is a fucking beast, including you. So stop feeling like the victim and start believing that shit about yourself," Vivian says.

The idea makes me smile and butterflies take off in my stomach. Maybe she is right. Maybe I could get my fairytale ending after all. I always thought Keegan was my dream come true. Maybe I was wrong. I *was* obviously is more the case. What is the worst that could happen if I reached out and took what I wanted? After all, Vivian is right—I survived The Chamber. Only the strong can survive and I am beginning to believe that I am strong. Vivian has no idea what she has done. Being with her is every bit as much a path to healing as Miles is, because she lived my nightmares.

"You are right! I am a beast. I can have what I want and I deserve to have it! Fuck Keegan. He didn't deserve me, but I sure know who does," I say and wrap my sister into the biggest hug of gratitude. "Thank you. I love you so much."

"I love you too!" she says and we are wiping tears from our eyes. Then we are busting up with laughter.

I never realized how healthy spending time with each other could be for us both.

"Did I just create a monster?" she asks as we start walking again. "I mean, you're not going to attack Miles the next time you see him, are you?"

I roll my eyes at her and giggle. "I mean, I don't see how any part of that would be a bad idea, but no. I'm going to stop second-guessing myself around him though. That is for sure."

Her smile is parental and proud, "You go, girl."

We bump shoulders gently.

I love Vivian. Always have. She was one of the strong ones inside The Chamber. Mason named her Flame because even he saw the fight in her. Some of her strong is definitely rubbing off.

"We need shoes," Vivian says.

OKAY SO I have one thing to say: the shoe salesmen must think we are crazy because we must try on every brand of shoes in Nieman's before we decide. I choose a pair of over-four-inch silver Louboutins with a laser-cut peep-toe.

My choice is tame in comparison to Vivian's. "You are going to break your neck with those shoes, love," I warn.

"Please, I can handle these." She waves me away with her hand. "Besides, Dominic is six-three, you're five-eight, and Miles is at least six-two. I'm the only shorty at a measly five-six, and I am stretching that." She giggles.

"How high is that heel?" I ask the man helping us.

"Six inches," he says.

"Vivian! You are going to kill yourself!"

"I'll take them!" she says. She walks around in her new silver and black, angel leather Gucci sky-high pumps. Even I have to give her credit for strutting so well.

"Now I can be a giant like the rest of you!" she teases.

We ring up our purchases. "I'm going to buy you those ridiculous albeit sexy shoes so that if you do manage to kill yourself it won't be considered suicide," I say, handing the cashier my card and laughing at my own joke. "By the way, I'm only two inches taller than you, perhaps two and a half," I tease, remembering that she fibbed on her exact height.

WE MEET up with the guys in the room. Seeing Dominic and Vivian inside our suite feels so comfortable to me. Like home. Growing up with a houseful is all I have ever known—aunties, uncles, cousins, family friends, and noise. I will chat with Miles and see if he would be okay with them staying with us for a while. Seeing how we are going to be training together anyway it seems the most convenient and fun idea.

Exhausted from shopping we decide to take naps. Miles takes his place next to me, because he doesn't want me to have a nightmare any more than I do.

"Can I ask you a couple of favors?" I say, my words sluggish because I am about to allow sleep to take me over.

"Anything," he says, moving closer to me.

We are facing each other. I could lie next to this man for the rest of my life. "First question, can Vivian and Dominic stay in the second bedroom for a while? I hate to ask, but I really need to be around my sister right now."

"Absolutely."

I smile.

He smiles. I wonder if he knows what his smile does to me?

"Second and last question. Can you let your guard down for one night and party with me? Like, get drunk with me?"

He leans in closer. "I can't think of anything I'd want to do more. I will be right back." He hops out of bed and jogs out of the room. He returns fifteen minutes later.

"Everything okay?" I ask, sitting up in bed.

His smile is breathtaking. "I guess it's a good thing we never unpacked our new clothes, because we're switching rooms," he says.

"When?" I ask.

"Now. You can nap in the new room."

"Okay." I don't ask questions. I trust him emphatically.

OUR NEW ROOM is several floors higher than the previous. It is a mega-suite with four bedrooms and nearly three-thousand square feet of living space. Enough room for Vivian and Dominic, Miles and me, *and* Jonathan and Mitch. Our personal items arrive shortly after us.

"This is amazing," I say to Miles when we lie down on our new bed in our much larger room. "Thank you so much, for everything."

"Anything, anytime," he says.

I can't resist. I fold myself into his arms. He doesn't pull or push me away. Instead he wraps his arms around me and kisses the top of my head.

"You nap now. You are going to need your energy to keep up with me on the dance floor." I know he's trying to lighten the mood. He must feel it too.

My heart is mending, with every inch of it that he takes up residence in. "I accept that challenge. But I should warn you, love— before I became a model I was a competitive dancer," I say, and giggle when his hand smacks his forehead in premature defeat.

"You know I trained the Jabbawockeez," he says.

"Whatever. Go to sleep, Miles."

"Anything for you, Miss O'Malley."

THE GUYS REACT JUST as we expected them to. They are shocked, awed, and I believe a little worried. Dominic is the first to speak up.

"Oh my damn, baby. You look ravishing."

Vivian twirls. "Why, thank you." She is wearing an Alexis Rustam black and white lace minidress, with long, sheer sleeves and a higher than mid-thigh scalloped hem. Oh, and best not forget her six-inch Gucci pumps. Her black hair is cascading down her back in big sexy waves. My sister is gorgeous.

Miles walks up to me and twirls me around, then leans close to my ear. In my four-inch heels I am only a couple inches shorter than him. "So did you want me to dance with you or spend the evening fighting off guys? Because you nearly stopped my heart in this dress."

Who needs cheek blush when you have an amazing man paying you compliments like that? "This little thing, love?" I say and stand back, astonished.

"Little is right. And sexy, that's another word for that dress," he says, assessing me from head to toe. The smile on his face registers that he likes what he sees.

Wow, I knew when I picked out this little mid-thigh Halston

Heritage one-shoulder embellished faux-wrap silver dress with my silver Louboutins he would like it, but I think he more than likes it.

"You look pretty damn snazzy yourself, love." He is wearing black dress pants and a charcoal dress shirt with a sheen, almost like we planned it.

"Do you know how much I love when you call me love?" he asks, his eyes all smiley and twinkly.

We are falling in love. I can feel it. It's not any big thing. It's a bunch of little things, like stolen glances, endearments, warm touches, or marveling at the many things we have in common. The biggest reason I know that I am in this bubble of newfound love with Miles is because I know that he wants the best for me. He wants me to be strong and confident, and most of all he wants me to be myself.

I should have known back in Ireland that he was special. I felt it the first day I met him. I knew it at the coffee shop, and now here he is, mine for the taking if I am smart enough to reach out and grab for what I want. "I do now," I say, my lashes fluttering, my cheeks warming.

Dominic looks equally chic in black dress pants and a burgundy dress shirt. With our bodyguards in tow, we are ready to go out.

First stop: the Whiskey Down. We order bottle service, and enjoy very strong whiskey and fine company. When we are sufficiently buzzed, we head to Hakkasan restaurant for a much needed dinner. We are ushered inside without wait because the guys made reservations for four and two—our bodyguards at a very nearby table. I love the effort the guys make to cast the illusion that Mitch and Jonathan are not with us, that our lives are normal, that we are just on a double date. How I wish the last part were true. Is it wrong to pretend that it is for one night?

Dinner is amazing. Every single moment: hanging out with my sister; the way Miles caresses my arm or grazes my leg—I'm sure each time is by accident or a platonic endearment, but for me they are the moments that add to this newfound bliss that I am allowing into my life.

The restaurant is chic and tropical at the same time, with ambient lighting, gorgeous latticework, and mood-altering colors. The food, a Cantonese-inspired masterpiece.

Catching Miles watching me, lighting up my heart with each smile, is Christmas, my birthday, and every special occasion of my life rolled up into one.

Best night ever.

Next stop: dancing.

The Ling Ling Room is the perfect-sized venue for us. The other room is an EDC explosion—I would be on sensory overload for sure. The guys secured us a VIP booth. Perfect. There are bottles of spirits and mixes on our table awaiting us. Our security has posted themselves around our booth, standing at the ready, making us look more important than we actually are. Which on a night like this is actually fecking cool.

"Let's toast!" I shout above the music.

A scantily clad woman pours drinks for us. I expect her to flirt with the guys, but she doesn't. She is all business.

"To new beginnings!" I shout.

"To sisters!" Vivian shouts.

Dominic takes his turn. "To finding the woman you can't live without!"

"To all of what you guys said!" Miles says.

We all down our shots, followed by a variety of reactions to the strength of the liquor. I cough, Vivian shakes her head repeatedly, and the guys both shout.

"Again!" I say. We take three strong shots in succession, and I can feel them *all*. My head is sufficiently swirling and my inhibitions are down.

"Let's go dance," Vivian shouts close in my ear.

I nod with excitement.

The dance floor is really a small space in close proximity to our booth. The song the DJ is spinning is a sexy hip hop song with lots of bass. Vivian and I dance together, moving our hips in that sexual way that makes guys go crazy. I am so happy that I chose to wear my hair down in soft fiery waves that fall to the middle of my back.

When I dare a glance over at Miles, his seductive gaze tells me he is enjoying the show.

"I think he really likes you, Maeve!" Vivian shouts over the music.

"I hope so!" I shout back. My smile says it all for me. I have it worse than bad.

We're continuing our slow gyrations on the dance floor when two very attractive guys approach us, asking us to dance. Both with chocolate brown hair and fair skin, and model good looks. Though I *have* had a lot to drink, so my assessment of their looks may be off. We attempt to dismiss them, but they persist and actually have the audacity to start dancing with us. Only a couple seconds go by before four turns to six as Miles and Dominic make their approach.

"Excuse me, gentlemen, but these ladies are with us," Dominic shouts, his deep voice booming over the slow, gentler song.

"Calm down, man, we are just dancing with these beautiful ladies," one of the guys says.

"Yeah, man, no harm," the other guy says. "You should never leave girls this hot on the dance floor alone." He smirks.

Oh my goodness, are they insane? Miles and Dominic are big, dangerous guys who just laid a claim to us. We are with them. No doubt alcohol has made them braver and stupid. We tell these assholes to bugger off and they refuse. I don't want a fight on my perfect night.

Just as our guys step forward to probably demolish these two insignificant jerks, Vivian wraps her arms around Dominic and smashes her lips into his, telling them that she is his. In a brazen move on my part, I wrap my arms around Miles. I don't kiss him, though every fiber in my soul wants me to. He isn't mine, and even liquored up I know I need to respect the boundary line he has drawn, even though everything about him blurs that line. My lips are dangerously close to his. I know he would taste divine. He smells edible. *Mmm.* Could I somehow turn the tides and make him mine? With him I already feel as though I can face anything, and I have only had one day of training.

We sway to the music. The idiots who wouldn't leave obviously get the hint because they disappear, leaving the four of us on the dance floor.

"You promised me a dance battle," Miles says close to my ear.

"I'm kinda liking doing this," I say. I don't want to not be in his arms for any reason. I glance over at Vivian and Dominic and she has come out of her six-inch heels. She is holding them in her hands while she dances and they look like they can be used as a weapon.

"Yeah, I'm enjoying this too," Miles whispers in my ear.

I may not be able to kiss him when I want, but I just had three strong shots, and we are about to have another. I pull him to our booth and pour two healthy shots. No toasting—we down them—and I pull him back onto the dance floor and show him exactly how I feel about him. If he doesn't reciprocate I can just use the excuse that I was drunk. The way Miles holds onto to me as we grind and move to the music tells a different story. If I didn't know any better, I would say that he wants me too.

The four of us take a seat when it gets so crowded that it feels like they turned the heat up. Thankful for our booth, Miles and I snuggle in the corner of one of the sofas.

"Maeve, do you have any idea how beautiful you are?" he asks.

"No, tell me." *Please tell me.*

"When I first laid eyes on you I knew that it was going to be a challenge to do my job. I wanted to walk away, because I didn't just want to protect you that day. I wanted you to be mine. In my business that is not the best way to begin protecting someone," Miles confesses.

Wow, that is a confession that I will replay over and over.

"How could you feel that way seeing me for the first time?" Hearing his candor is sobering. I don't dare peel my eyes from his.

"There was something about you, more than your beauty. Something inside you dying to get out, a part of you I knew I wanted to meet. Even in that tiny moment I wanted more."

"And?" Butterflies are battling inside me.

"And what?"

"Are you happy with your decision? Have you met this part of me?"

He leans in closer to me. "Can I try something?"

"Anything." I can barely think straight with him so close to me. My head feels swirly. That is a funny word...*swirly*. I repeat it in my head until it sounds foreign. I have a feeling what he wants, though I can't be sure. But I would give him anything.

We are face to face, so close that our lips are nearly touching. There is no music playing in my background. I'm sure it is there—we *are* in a club—but the only sound I am aware of is our deep breaths. I want to close the distance, put my lips to his as I have in my dreams, but I don't dare. Miles grabs the back of my hair and does what I am too afraid to do. When his lips meet mine it is all I can do not to pass out. What starts off as a soft, tender kiss ignites into the passion and desire we both feel for each other. I want to climb into his lap, but don't. I want to lie onto my back and take him with me, but I won't. This is his dance to lead.

His hands warm the small of my back as he pulls me closer to him. Our lips and tongues devour each other. He breaks away from kissing me and I feel his breathing in my ear, sending fiery sensations down my body. *Oh my.*

"To answer your question, I am falling in love with her," he whispers.

I pull back and look at him. Did I hear him correctly? We are locked eye to eye. I bite down on my lower lip. I do not take my eyes away from his. Then I smile. "Best thing I've heard all day...I mean, it's wonderful to know that I am not the only one feeling that way," I say. "I am feeling more and more like her everyday. She is the very best part of me and I have enjoyed her presence. I kinda hope she stays around." I say, and this time it is my turn. I take Miles's hand and pull him off the couch. "Stay right here. Don't move."

He nods in agreement.

I walk over to Vivian and Dominic. "We are headed back to the room. We may be back, though I doubt it." My face splits into a smile.

"Take one of the guys with you." Dominic orders.

"Okay," I say.

"You two have fun!" Vivian squeals, squeezing my hand.

I fold into Miles's arms and lead him to our room, though I don't make my intentions known. Mitch follows close behind. Mitch slips the access key into the elevator and the three of us step inside when it pings and opens. I separate from Miles once inside. I want to see him. Really see him before I make him mine. I'm sure he believes the distance has something to do with Mitch and the three of us traveling in the confines of this mechanical box.

I stand on the opposite end and watch.

My chest rises and falls with haste.

I see lust in his eyes as he watches me.

My lids heavy with desire, I catch a moan before it escapes me.

I may be unsure of so much around me, but not this. I am a graduate of The Chamber and I have become skilled in the art of pleasurable sex in a way that would make Miles's head explode. As he will soon see.

The tension in the elevator is so thick, it feels as though ten more bodies are riding with us. Sex slams into me, pulling me closer to Miles. When is this fecker going to reach our floor because I am so wet they are going need a mop for this floor. Miles undoes his top button, telling me he is having a hard time breathing.

Yes. Just wait until you are buried deep inside me. We may need to call an ambulance when I am done with you. My legs wobble when we finally reach our floor. For all of my bravado my nerves are starting to get to me. I mean, this is Miles.

Mitch probably wants to get out of the way because he opens the door in haste. I pull Miles by the hand toward our room. I am already undoing my dress when the door closes behind us, standing in front of Miles, wearing only a strapless black lacy push-up bra, matching lace panties and my heels.

I am sex.

I am raw passion.

I wait for him to undress. He regards me with a look of lust and admiration, then like an answered prayer he unbuttons his shirt and lets it fall to the floor. His pants follow. Miles's body is every bit as spectacular as I imagined. Chiseled and grooved in all the right places, with that perfect vee that leads to where I can only imagine my new heaven must be. His full erection is *everything*. I want him like nothing I have ever wanted in my life so far.

"Are you sure?" he asks, breathless in want.

"More than anything."

"Are you drunk? I don't want to make love to you tonight only to have you wake up filled with regret. If I make love to you tonight, you will be mine by morning."

"I think I was yours the moment you got on the plane with me. This works both ways. The moment I sink that loveliness between your legs into my mouth, you belong to me."

I watch as his face registers shock before he can cover it up and he swallows hard. "Deal. I'm yours," he promises.

That is all I needed to hear. "Then you should hold on." I strut across the room and peel off his boxer briefs and set his erection free. It is every bit the specimen I expected. Beefy, the way I had hoped, with a length that promises to please. I sink to my knees. I stare up into his eyes, mine full of the promises we just made. Miles's eyes are wide with amazement. I open my mouth and take just the tip inside. I savor the tip with my tongue, round and round until he is moaning his pleasure. Then I beginning sucking, taking his entire length into my mouth, over and over.

"Maeve, ohh, Maeve. This feels amazing, but I'm not coming like this," he pulls me to stand. We lock eyes. "Damn, girl. That was fucking amazing."

His lips crash into mine, both hands holding my face. I can't breathe I am so overcome with joy being able to share this moment with someone like this.

"I love you, Maeve," he says between kisses. His hands skillfully undo my bra. He breaks my kiss and he sinks to his knees. First, he removes my shoes. Then his hands explore my bare skin, caressing. It is scintillating.

Moans escape and I don't stop them. I am nerve endings raw and exposed as he comes up and takes one of my nipples into his mouth. *Yess!* The he takes the other one into his mouth. His free hand cups my sex and a finger slips inside me, then two.

"I love you too!" I nearly come around his fingers. "I love you!"

"You are so wet and ready for me," he says.

"I want you so bad, love. Take me and make me yours."

Miles scoops me into his arms as if I weigh nothing and lays me onto the bed. My chest is rising and falling, while he watches me for an agonizing time. My legs open, revealing the prize awaiting him. He leaves me and goes into the bathroom. He emerges tearing open a condom package.

"Always carry those around?"

"Dominic bought them for me from the gift shop as a hint of what he thought we should be doing in our spare time."

I shake my head. "Please, no. I've got that part covered, I promise. I want to feel all of you."

He tosses it and joins me on the bed. His lips find mine again as he sinks deep inside me. We fit perfectly together. Miles pushes farther inside me and I thrust my hips forward to receive all that he has to give me.

"You feel amazing, Maeve," Miles moans. "Look at me," he asks.

I gaze into his eyes. I can see lust and pleasure, but mostly I see care and love. I don't break eye contact as he continues to push in and pull out of me, his erection hard and fulfilling. I feel the tension building inside me, overcome by the excitement of finally making love to someone of my choosing, someone I want to be with more than air.

I push at his shoulder and indicate that I want to be on top. Miles rolls us over and I sit up straight and stare down my nose at him, my lids hooded with desire. I don't move. Instead I contract and release my walls around him.

His moans tell me that he likes what I am doing. With my eyes never leaving his I begin to roll my hips. His erection feels amazing inside me. I am so full of him that I want to cry and laugh and scream from the feeling that is taking over.

Forward and backward.

Up and down.

Slow, delicious circles around his enormous cock. The look in his eyes and the moans escaping him tell me that he is about to reach his peak of excitement and I will be along for that ride with him. We both erupt in a glorious mountain of sensations, cries, moans, and love spasms. I collapse on his chest and I don't move an inch. His cock pulsates deliciously inside me. We are fast breaths, sweat, and pounding hearts.

"That was the most amazing thing I have ever experienced," Miles says breathlessly.

"I'd agree if I had the strength," I tease. He attempts to pull out, but I push closer to him. After all, I am still on top and have more control. "Don't you dare take my new best friend away from me. We are still getting acquainted."

Miles complies and a small, pleased laugh escapes his lips. We fall asleep in this way.

19

MILES: HAVING MY CAKE AND EATING IT TOO

*W*ould it be in poor form to propose to Maeve today? I answer my own question and the answer is yes. If I didn't think she would laugh in my face, I might just do it. I mean, I know Maeve is kind and she would let me down gently and never laugh, but the answer of course would be no. We barely know each other, and she has so much healing and growing to do as a person that it would be wrong. But after making love to her last night, I am convinced that there is no other woman on this planet for me but her. She is, in a word, everything. How can I want more?

She is smart, funny, creative, loving, sexy, and beautiful.

But, in the same breath, she is vulnerable, afraid, and in the middle of major healing. I already feel guilty for letting things go so far. How selfish am I? But then I have to remember what Dominic said to me—I can love her through this, and if I really love her I will want to protect her more than anything on this earth.

I can do this. I can love her and be in love with her, and I can train her to be lethal because of the love I have for her. I have no choice. The line has been crossed. The blurred lines have intertwined. We are a team.

But can I be with her again like I was last night? Is that fair to her?

Oh my goodness, I want it to be, because making love to her was the most spectacular thing that has ever happened to me. She became mine last night. And I take the best of care with what's mine.

It is hard to believe that Maeve and I could find love under these circumstances, but we have. I love her more than anything. My fear is that we moved to soon—she is hardly ready. Dominic encouraged me to move forward based on his life with Vivian. Vivian and Maeve may share The Chamber, but that is the extent of what they have in common. Maeve was fragile before her time at that evil place. Her problems began long before. I'm sure when Vivian came home things might not have been perfect but from what I understand, she had two very loving guys to choose from, not a douche-rocket of a fiancé and a world of judging faces.

I should have given her more time. But to step away from her now would be as good as rejecting her, and that is the opposite of what she needs. No one wants to hear *I'm leaving you for you, not me.* Even it were true, it would take time for them to understand the truth behind your words. In the beginning they would despise you. The only choice I have is to let her lead in the romance department. I will listen to her. Not her words, but her unspoken words to guide me.

Okay, I need to get out of my head, because overthinking is a man's worst enemy. My new vow is to take care of even her simplest desire.

Hunger, that should be her first desire this morning. I decide to grab breakfast for my girl. I order eggs, bacon, toast, and juice for us.

20

MAEVE: AM I DREAMING?

I wake earlier than usual, because my mind remembers what happened between Miles and me last night. Our promises to one another. The perfect puzzle fit that our lovemaking revealed. Was it real? I open my eyes one at a time and find myself alone in bed.

It was a fecking dream, wasn't it? No way something so amazing could have really happened to me.

It would have been the perfect ending to the most wonderful day. I am about to hop out of bed to go to the bathroom when the door to our room opens. Miles is standing in the opening. Cast in heavenly light from the living room, he regards me with a look so tender I can only blush.

"Good morning, beautiful. I brought breakfast. I thought you might be hungry after last night," he says, crossing the room.

So I didn't imagine last night.

I stretch my arms above my head. "Hi there," I say.

Miles crosses the room in haste and I am swept into his arms and our lips are entwined. I don't hesitate to peel his clothes off so that he is bare-muscled perfection in front of me. His erection is full when he sinks deep inside me. The feeling is everything. In and out he thrusts into me. We are sighs and moans. I grind my hips around in circles as that familiar feeling builds inside me. I nudge him to encourage him to roll over so I am atop. When I gaze down at him, the look in his eyes tells me only that he is in love. I don't move, he doesn't move. I contract my walls around him and his body flinches in pleasure each time.

"I love you," I say.

"I love you," he says.

Tears fall uncontrolled onto his chest and stomach. I trail my fingers through the grooves and sinews of his body, dragging my tears down. Then I lose myself in this moment. Grinding onto his cock as if it were a ride at the fair. I lift up and sink down over and over until we both come apart. The fiery sensations are powerful and wonderful, because Miles is the first man I have made love to in more than a year. I don't stop grinding after we come and it is driving him crazy. When I can no longer move I collapse on his chest. His arms envelop me.

I don't know how long we are asleep, but my noisy stomach wakes me. "I'm hungry now," I say.

"Well we will have to go get food, because I am sure what I got is cold."

We don't bother showering. We dress and head down in search of food.

21

MILES: EXHAUSTED

*T*his morning at breakfast she glowed and radiated love, and it was beautiful on her. She should always wear that shade of happy. We shared a plate at the buffet as only a couple experiencing new love can. We each had to eat with one hand because we couldn't keep the other ones to ourselves. It was nice. Older couples watching us didn't seem to see color, only a young, happy couple in love.

We meet with Dominic and Vivian at a private warehouse that is equipped with space for gymnastics and boxing. We warm them up with running. For Dominic and me this is easy, but the girls look like they are going to kill us. When we hit the center floor, Maeve is out of breath, clutching her side and says, "There's more?" I can't help but laugh and nod. The look on her face is that of a toddler who was told they couldn't have a toy or dessert, and I want to kiss the wrinkle between her eyes. *Adorable.*

We take them through a conditioning routine that we expect them to eventually commit to memory. This way they can do it anywhere.

After conditioning we take them into the boxing ring and work on some simple kicks and strikes. When the girls are sufficiently beat, we take them to grab lunch. Maeve is so tired she asks for a smoothie so she doesn't have to chew.

The girls crash the second we get back to the room, so I head into the living room area to watch TV with Dominic.

"I think I made a huge mistake with Maeve," I say when he hands me a cold beer and flops down on the other couch.

"Why, man?"

"I think it was too soon. She needs more time to get herself together, and now I pushed her into intimacy. It's only gonna confuse her," I say.

"How do you know this isn't exactly what she needs?"

I take a swig of my beer and think about what he is saying.

"You love her, right?" he continues.

"I do. I love her. But I don't know if she should depend on me this way, before she even knows how to depend on herself," I say and let out the breath I am holding.

"Look, I get what you are saying. But the way I see it, as long as what you do with her is out of love, you can't go wrong. She will learn all this about herself...it just might take longer 'cause you fucked up and blurred the lines," he teases.

I throw a sofa pillow at him. "You ass!" He was the one who was extra-encouraging me.

Dominic laughs.

Fucker.

Maybe he is right. Only time will tell. I know one thing—it is nice to have them on this journey with us.

22

"Uh, did we really sign up for this shite?" I ask Vivian while we do our seven-billionth squat. "Because if we did, once we are ripped and trained we should kick our own asses!"

I have never worked so hard in my entire life. We run through this freaking conditioning routine daily. Today we are doing it in our hotel suite on our own while the fecking guys just watch.

"I hate them! We should kick their asses," she says and we glare at the guys who only laugh harder at us.

After we go through this brutal routine—which I have to admit is reshaping parts of me; I notice I am not as soft as I was in my legs and arms—we are heading back to the gun range on Blue Diamond Road. The guys in there are really cool and the big German Shepherd always greets me. The guys said that Vivian and I have taken very well to shooting handguns. I won't say that I like guns more than before, but I definitely have a respect for them. At some point in our training we are going to experience what we should do if someone pulls a gun on us. *Scary.*

～

AS ALWAYS, after training we are treated. This afternoon we are going to be spoiled at the spa. Which Vivian and I really need for our sore everything.

"This is the part I love—the special reward for our hard work," Vivian says.

I don't look over at her because my eyes are covered with cucumber. We are wrapped up like mummies. "Me too. If I could, I would like to just do this part of the training," I say.

Vivian giggles. "Good luck getting either one of them to agree to that."

"A girl can try, right?"

"Yep, she can. Speaking of a girl trying... I notice things steaming up with you and Miles," Vivian says.

"Truthfully, I don't know what we were waiting for. We are really good together. I just hope it lasts." I say my fears aloud.

Silence.

"Listen, we can't predict the future. If anyone knows that it's you and me... The only thing we can do is live in each moment and hope for the best future we can get. Hell, a bus could run us over after this beautiful spa day."

I sigh. "That is an awful thought, Vivian," I say.

"Doesn't make it a lie."

"Sure doesn't."

We sit in oversized, comfy chairs like lumps of formless clay, relaxed by our numerous treatments. There are cold and hot dipping pools in front of us, but I am too loose to move. Instead, we sip cucumber and lemon water and have an array of teas and fresh fruit to snack upon.

"Do you think about it often?" I don't have the say what *it* is. I know that Vivian is one of the strong from our time in The Chamber. Does she have bad dreams? Does she remember vivid details like I do?

"More often than I care to. I wish there a pill I could take to help me forget. What about you?"

"The nightmares are less frequent. I don't know, since I came to

Vegas I have felt better. Being with you has been the best kind of therapy. A real sisterhood. I guess I could really begin to heal if I knew that evil place didn't exist and the man responsible was behind bars."

We both sigh. "I know. I feel awful knowing the things that are taking place there right now. Dominic has a plan though. It scares the shit out of me, but he is hell-bent on bringing that maniac to his knees," she says.

"Scary is only the half of it. I wish him all the luck. He must know what he is up against. If you guys need anything let me know. I mean, a fat lot of good I can be, but who knows what you might need along the way."

"I love you, Maeve," Vivian says.

"I love you too," I say. "Hey, when's the wedding?"

"August, and you and Miles better be there. I want you in my wedding."

"I wouldn't miss it for the world!"

23

MAEVE: FEELING THE HEAT

*J*n a rare gesture of kindness the guys give us two days off from training! Let me clarify—they are two days in a row. It shouldn't feel like hitting the lottery but it does. My body changes are a direct reflection of the training. If I wanted to go back to modeling, it would have to be for fitness companies at this point. My shoulders are missing the softness they once had, and it has been replaced by lines that were never drawn before. My abs have changed too. Well, another clarification. I used to have a flat *stomach*. Now I have abs, like a four-pack! I also don't hate running as much as I did before, except for the fact that this city is too hot for most outdoor activities.

We decide to spend the day at the pool. Again, one of the guys has the forethought to secure a cabana for us. It's the middle of June and by late morning it is already a scorcher. Vivian is rocking a tiny red bikini and I am wearing a black one. I am so proud of Vivian that she can wear anything red after suffering that color for an entire year in The Chamber. And she wears it like a badge. The guys both opt for Hawaiian-print board shorts.

There are half-naked gorgeous women everywhere, showing off the bodies they worked so hard on during the year. Most, anyway. I am sure that some of these sculpted bodies before us were purchased. A chisel here, a tuck there.

"I don't want to complain about your city, Vivian, but you enjoy baking out here like this? It really feels like I am on the center rack in the oven set to four-hundred-fifty degrees." I fan myself but it isn't working.

Vivian laughs. A waitress comes and offers us drinks. I order all the water she can carry on her tray, and Miles coats me with another spray of sunscreen. Did I mention I am fair with freckles? *Shade, please.*

"You get used to the weather. I love it!" Vivian says.

"Oh I am bringing you to Ireland, my friend. The weather there is a dream!"

"Come on, Maeve, it's not that hot!"

Miles leans past me. "Are you insane? I fear we might be in the depths of hell," Miles teases.

We all look to Dominic to get his take on the Vegas heat. "Don't look at me. This shit is ridiculous! At least back home we have afternoon rains to cool us down. Vegas has the nerve to have a breeze in the summer. That just feels like someone turned on a blow dryer and put it in your face," Dominic says.

"You guys are all wimps! For all your training, you get whipped by Mother Nature!" Vivian laughs at her joke.

"Don't front on Mother Nature. She is a bad bitch," Miles says.

We all laugh, but anyone who has seen an earthquake, hurricane, flood, or tornado can attest to her power.

The waitress comes back with waters for me, beers for the guys, and a martini for Vivian. Our friends Jonathan and Mitch are with us today. Anytime Miles and Dominic plan to drink, their extra pair of eyes appear. I don't mind them much. They are nice and very professional. Their presence does give off the impression that we are more important than we are. Not that we aren't important people— everyone is. I mean in a political, celebrity, or social way. Their presence screams, *whoever these people are they are worthy of personal protection.*

Even with the shade the heat is exhausting. I watch the drunken fun that people around me are having. Still, I keep with the water. I know myself—if I drink in this heat, I will only be sleepy.

At one point I follow Miles to the pool because he promises it will cool me off. We walk in from the beach entry and keep walking until we are in waist deep. The water is cool and refreshing. I sink under, so that I am drenched from head to toe. Did I mention that Miles never lets go of my hand the entire time we are in the pool? Without being prompted, I use my second pair of eyes and take in my surrounding now that we have changed locations. Something Miles has beaten into me. *Always reassess. Even if you stay in the same place for a time, people are constantly on the move.*

Vivian is sitting on Dominic's lap under our cabana. Jonathan and Mitch are sipping water to keep hydrated and their heads are on a subtle swivel. There are too many people in the pool to count at the moment, most drinking some sort of alcohol, enjoying *this heat*. No immediate threats in the area.

Miles smiles proudly and his lips graze my cheek. "I see you," he says.

"Trained by the best," I say.

WHEN WE GET BACK to the room, I crash. No shower. We are going out to dinner tonight and I am wiped from doing nothing at all but spending a day at the pool. I feel eighty years old. I don't dream. I rarely have nightmares anymore. I can feel myself getting better, stronger. My only hope is that the reason has something to do with me, and not because of Miles alone. It is hard to tell what is the truth in that query because I never gave myself the chance to go it alone. I hope I have had something to do with my growth, because I would be a fool to give a man the power again.

How could I ever tell? How would I ever know?

WE GET SHOWERED and dressed to go out. I am relieved that this isn't a super-dressy night. I am still exhausted from the pool so I don a sleeveless floral romper and sandals. Barely there make-up and my hair in natural waves, because I didn't want the heat of styling products. Everyone is going casual tonight, and of course Jonathan and Mitch accompany us. We decide to hit the Linq to ride the giant Ferris wheel and we eat at Guy Fieri's famous and delicious restaurant.

I am on cloud nine with the way my life has turned out. Never in a million years would I have imagined any of this. Spending time with my Chamber sister? Insane, right? I never thought I would see her again. Vivian mentioned that she has spoken with Sapphire, Sunshine, and Violet—I mean Emmanuella, Whitney, and Brinley—since our release. That is unbelievable and wonderful. I never thought we'd be in touch but the bond we have is undeniable. Perhaps I should reach out to my roommate, Scarlet. The monster named her Raven inside.

I never thought that I would fall in love either. Life is crazy! You start out heading down one road and the terrain can change under your feet. Keegan was a life of dirt and gravel, sharp pointy rocks that bite at the bottoms of your feet, requiring careful thought with each step. But Miles, he is green grass and gorgeous waters. A life with him is breathtaking views, frolicking skips across the green, rolling pasture. I am not saying he is perfect, for no one is. But with Miles I can be the real me. I already fell in love with Miles, and I am ready to fall in love with Maeve.

As I walk with Miles, our arms around each other, I realize that I am not ready to run through the lush grass with him. I don't deserve to be drenched under the beautiful waterfall, Miles by my side. I am still a work in progress and the rest of this journey I must go alone. If I don't I will never know if he alone is responsible for my healing or if I had something to do with it. I owe it to myself to see this through on my own, and if Miles is in line at the end of my journey like he said he would be, he will only love me more for my strength and bravery.

And most important—I will love me more too.

24

MAEVE: INNER STRENGTH

*W*e had so much fun tonight. We rode the High Roller twice! Guy's restaurant was better than promised. Vivian got sunburned! I hadn't noticed it before—I was too exhausted. I don't know what she was thinking. She may not have freckles but she is as pale as I am.

When we retire to our rooms for the night I prepare myself for our conversation. I change into my sleep clothes—boy shorts and a tank top. Miles is distracting in plaid pajama bottoms and no shirt. So tempting.

I flop myself down on the center of the bed and sit yoga style with my legs crossed.

Miles is lying on his back. His hand finds my knee and he begins to caress it. "Hi, beautiful."

"Hi, beautiful yourself," I say. "I wanted to talk to you about something serious and I don't think you are going to like it," I blurt out.

He sits up in bed. Not in alarm or concern, but with interested eyes. "I'm listening," he says.

I let out a long breath. "I want to start off by saying thank you for everything you have done for me. I want to tell you that I am in the deepest of love with you and I could easily spend the rest of my life with a man like you." I pause. "No, not a man like you. You, Miles. I could spend the rest of my life with you. I want to do that, you know. Grow old in your arms, still able to kick your butt!"

I laugh but it doesn't come out right because I am nervous. Miles takes my hand and caresses it. Only love in his gaze.

I continue. "I have to return home. Alone. I don't want to break up with you. I don't want to leave you. But I can't tell if my growth is because of me or all due to you...and I can't be the person for you until I know for sure that I only need me to get through this life."

Miles pulls me into a warm hug. His arms caress me. "Well, I can't say that I didn't see this coming. I understand that this is an important part of your journey, the last leg. I love you too much to do anything but support you."

I squeeze him so tight. Tears fall from my eyes. "Will you wait for me?"

"No."

Shocked, I pull away from him. "What? Why not?" Fear courses through my body. How can I do this without knowing I will still have him in my life?

"Maeve, if there's one thing I know about life it's that it could change on a dime. When you are ready I could be anywhere or nowhere at all. You could find that your feelings for me were a matter of the circumstances that you were in and you used me to get you through tough times. I am a realist. You do owe it to yourself to do this. I believe it is time. And I will bid you farewell, best wishes, and we will see what the future holds," he says.

All I can do is nod in agreement again. I am afraid for the first time in a couple of months, but I can do this.

I booked my flight home while I was in the bathroom changing for bed. I leave in the morning. Miles wraps me in his arms and we fall asleep holding onto each other for what could be the last time.

25

MILES: LOSING MY GIRL

$\mathcal{I}$ am not surprised by what Maeve revealed to me this evening. I respect her for the decision she has made. When she is in a deep sleep I slip my arm out from underneath her and head to the living room. It is so strange to think that all of this is going to end. I pop open a beer and sit back and watch a silent television. I lied when I said I wouldn't wait for her. I had to. For one thing, if she knew I was going to be there for her at the end, then her leaving proves nothing to her about her strength and character because me waiting in the cut is a sure thing—she can take comfort in that knowledge. This way it's all on her, all up to her. I could see the fear in her eyes and yet she was still strong enough to stick with her decision. I am so proud of her.

Of course I am going to wait for her. I am in love with every inch of her, body and soul. She is my everything. I have never felt the way I feel about her for any woman in my entire life. I risked everything for her and now I put the faith of our love and our life together in her. I believe that she is truly in love with me, but she doesn't know it yet because of the circumstances. I can only hope that she will come back to me. My faith in us says she will, but I am not one hundred percent sure.

THE NEXT MORNING, we all wake early. Vivian is upset that Maeve is leaving. But Maeve promises to make the trip to California in August for the wedding. The four of us hit the buffet for breakfast. I hold Maeve's hand in line. I hold her hand when we are eating. I hold her hand when we leave. I want her to know every step of the way that she is loved no matter what.

We walk her as far as we can at the airport.

"I love you so much and I am so proud of you," I say.

"I love you too, Miles, with everything in here." She touches her chest over her heart. Then her lips smash into mine. I dip my tongue into her mouth and pull her as close to me as possible. Tears threaten to fall from my eyes, but I fight them. I can tell my eyes are misty. When we separate her face is wet.

"Head on a swivel, baby. Every scene tells a story. Read your environment," I remind her.

She nods and wipes her eyes. Next she hugs Dominic.

"You be safe out there. Remember, eye contact shows what?"

"Strength and confidence." She repeats what we have told them so many times.

He pats her head and smiles like a proud older brother.

Vivian wipes her eyes and rushes into Maeve's arms. They both sob. This has been so good for them both.

"You better get your shit together and be back for the wedding! And if you see that asshat, Keegan, you beat the shit out of him! You hear me?" she demands.

Fuck me! I am going to have a fucking nervous breakdown. I am just sending the woman I love into the woods for the wolves and bears. What if she falls apart under the pressure? What if she tries to hurt herself again? Fucking Keegan. I need to call in some reinforcements, watch her from afar. If something happens to her I will never forgive myself.

"Miles, I will be fine," she says, obviously sensing my fear at the mere mention of Keegan's name. "That fecker isn't a thought in my mind. Besides, I have been trained by the two best fighters around," she says and flexes her bicep. It protrudes, the cutest little bump ever, but she is pretty damned strong.

"Okay," I say and attempt to calm myself, but it is taking everything in me not to hop on that plane with her.

Again, sensing my apprehension, she takes off and turns back toward our pathetic group. "I love you all! I will miss you all!"

The love of my life vanishes into security and I let go. I know it isn't supposed to be manly when a guy cries but I don't give a fuck about society and its dumb-ass norms. My heart is fucking broken *and* I have to trust that nothing happens to the most important person in my entire world, *and* she is going to be across international waters!

Vivian and Dominic guide me to a row of seats and offer me comfort.

"I know exactly how you feel, bro. I went through the same type of thing with Vivian. She will come back to you. She loves you."

"Dominic is right. She and I have talked so many times. You are in her heart, her bones. She'll be back, she just needs time."

I nod my head and hope to god that they are right. My heart will not beat the same without her in my life.

I can't believe I was strong enough to say goodbye to Miles. If that is not a show of some gumption on my part, I don't know what is. I have never been the girl with the balls. Out of my friends, Ciara was always the ballsy one. In The Chamber that honor was bestowed on Sapphire, Flame, and Raven, or Emmanuella, Vivian, and Scarlet. No one would ever add my name to that list until now. But the funny thing is I don't even really care what list I land on anymore. I gave up the love of my life in pursuit of finding myself and I don't give a flying feck what anyone thinks about me anymore.

This is the second time that I am returning home to Ireland. This time is different because I have no false hopes, no delusions that this place or the people within the walls of my home can cure me. That, I learned, is no one else's job but mine. My healing isn't dependent on friends, family, or a man.

I owed it to myself to finally open my eyes to see that.

To stand on my own two feet.

I'm not saying Miles didn't help, because he did. Him wanting me and showing me that my experiences don't define me was a colossal part of my journey. Still, I associated my healing with him, and while he is an amazing man, I was wrong because I needed to make sure that my healing was ultimately because of me.

Our breakup, though initiated by me, was mutual. He was incredible even in the face of losing me, proving once again that he is the perfect man for me. And still I was strong enough to say goodbye.

We always knew there were lines we shouldn't have crossed, and I am thankful that Miles cares enough for me to help me draw the lines back where they were. Making love to him was also valuable at the time, because before him the only sexual relationships I had besides with Keegan were at The Chamber. To experience such love and tenderness with a man who loves me was like bathing in healing waters. We set out to keep our relationship platonic and failed epically—thank goodness for that, because I needed every tender touch, every caress, every loving smile and kiss on my journey.

The choices I made to leave him and all that he offers me behind will be my power now and forever. Sure, I miss him. I miss him so much that it hurts. But this isn't about him, it's about me. I will forever be grateful for all that he taught me, and I will always love him, but it feels fecking amazing to finally fall in love with myself.

Maeve standing on her own two feet.

Maeve not second-guessing her choices.

Maeve living a life without fear.

My time in Las Vegas will always be special to me. Though it wasn't long, I am a pretty good shot with a handgun, I have a developing second sight, and with two months of intensive self-defense training from Miles and Dominic I am no longer afraid.

This time, no surprises. My folks know I am coming. Two months, that's how long my absence was this time. I use my key and open the door. It is the middle of the day so the twins are in school. They will be excited to see me, but I have kept in regular contact with them as well as my folks.

"Ma! Da! I'm home," I yell into the open space.

"In the kitchen, love," Ma's voice calls out to me.

Ma is busying herself at the stove and whatever she is cooking smells divine. I missed my ma. I do hope that she understands the purpose of my departure. "Hi, Ma. It smells delicious. You didn't have to go to the trouble of cooking for me," I say and wrap my arms around her with her back to me.

"Rubbish." She turns and hugs me. "My darling girl is home. Let me get a look at you," she says, stretching her arms out, pushing me arm's distance from her. "You look amazing, dear. I mean it," she says, squeezing my body in places. She doesn't say anything, but I know she feels the firmness under her hands.

I hug her again, but only so that I can steal a look into the pot.

"You get out of that pot this instant," she says, catching me.

"Chili?" I ask.

"Yes, chili."

"But you've never made chili before, Ma."

"Well," she says, motioning for me to have a seat with her at the table, "you're not the only one trying new things around here. I've been experimenting with dishes from all over the world. You would be surprised at how much the twins love Buffalo wings!"

I can't do anything but laugh. She is playing the part, but I can see that she is relieved that I am home.

"So how are you, love?"

"I'm actually a lot better. I realized that I am not this unlucky girl. Sure, the things that happened to me sucked and were awful, but I'm not the only one who has gone through shite, Ma. Miles taught me so much. I can really take care of myself. I'm not gonna stop my training either. I will be so lethal, people will want to hire me to protect them."

"Maeve!"

"What?!"

"That's what your security is for."

"Rubbish! I don't need random men walking around protecting me, Ma! I can stand up for myself now!" I should have known that I would be met with resistance on this. But I will not be accompanied by security this time. "Let Da know I'm home. I'm going to go see my friends."

"Maeve! Wait!"

I don't respond.

I haven't driven my car since I was taken. My little white two-door Audi is parked in its usual spot in the garage. I don't hop right in. Even though it's in my own garage, safe and tucked away, I use my second pair of eyes and assess. That is what Miles taught me—always take in my surroundings, and listen. Scan the nearby and the faraway. When I am satisfied that all is well I hop in.

I zip out onto the road and it feels amazing. I feel free.

I haven't been alone like this in forever. I'm not anxious or worried. For the first time in years I am happy in my skin. Not like Vegas. I was happy in Vegas too and I could have stayed in my little love bubble with Miles forever. This is different. I have no one else to attribute my current euphoric state to but me. I don't expect anyone to sweep in and save the day any longer. That's my job.

When I pull up to the Finnegan's pub in Dalkey I do what I am trained to do. I take in my scenery. A few parked cars, couples walking holding hands, a couple of men walking alone, and two packs of men walking in groups. The sky is typically cloudy, just the way I like it. I climb out of my car, hit the lock button on my key fob and reassess my surroundings as I walk around my car toward the sidewalk. A tall man of muscular build, with dark blond hair and two tattooed sleeves walks in my direction. The entrance to Finnegan's is about one hundred feet away. He is wearing Doc Martens, skinny jeans. I would guess his age close to mine. As he and I grow closer to crossing paths, I take the opportunity to glance into a storefront window. Miles taught me that storefront windows can be very telling. It allows you a larger scene grab without having to turn your head. For example, if several men were approaching me from different angles, I would see them before they were upon me. All of these things are automatic for me now. I don't really give them much thought, just a natural part of my travels. Satisfied that my surroundings are still clear, I continue forward. When my path crosses with the blond stranger, I make eye contact with him. Something the old me would have never done—I would have naturally averted my gaze. *Submissive.*

Not anymore.

"Hello, beautiful," he says.

"Hello," I say, and offer him a smile that says *I am going about my business; say no more to me.*

When I make it into the pub I see my girls already inside. I rush toward them. I have missed them so much.

"Where is your highly paid security force?" Ciara asks me.

"Gone. I don't need them," I say proudly.

"And Miles? You don't need him, either?" Saoirse asks.

Silence.

My friends are smart girls. They sit and wait me out.

"Okay, needs and wants. What are you asking me? I mean, of course I want him. I am in love with him," I admit.

"Oh my! I am so happy for you, Maeve," Ciara says.

"Me too. You deserve to fall in love with an amazing guy," Saoirse says.

I notice that my friends are careful not to bring up two subjects. "Listen, ladies, it has been a stellar year. I was released from being kidnapped, found out my ex-fiancé is a douche, and tried to off myself."

They share worried looks. I roll my eyes at both of them.

"If I can survive that, and I have, then I owe it to myself to not need anyone but myself. So I walked away from Miles. I had to. It wasn't healthy for me to go from loving the douche to falling for the next man that came along, especially since he rescued me. This right here is healthy, hanging with my girls," I say and we proceed to wrap ourselves in a big, loving hug.

Light floods the pub entrance and I am temporarily blind because it is so dark inside, and even on a cloudy day, it is much brighter outside. I can barely make out the forms of two men, but I can tell by the heavy steps that they are men. Once the door closes I take closer inventory of the new pub customers. Before I left I would have shite my pants seeing Keegan walk into this pub, but not today. I mean, I said I wanted to test my survival skills, and I guess the good Lord was thinking no time like the present.

"Well, as I live and breathe, if it isn't the poor unfortunate Irish girl and her gaggle of friends," Keegan calls out to me.

I only offer him a kind smile. I feel nothing toward him. Not anger or hate, not love or fear or even like. I feel nothing. I learned that if someone treats you like shite, you should treat them like they deserve to be treated. Like nothing.

"If I was truly unfortunate I would have actually married you, Keegan, so instead I think I will consider myself lucky, 'cause getting kidnapped saved me from a very unfortunate life with you," I shout back to him. The look on his face speaks volumes. He is shocked by my words. "Why don't you and your friend come and join us for a spell?"

My friends look at me like I have grown a third breast or something. I give them a look that says *trust me*, so they do.

Keegan and his friend take us up on the offer. My girls scoot onto the bench next to me, while the guys sit opposite us. Another thing I learned, when dealing with a potential enemy...barriers are good, and a large, heavy wooden table in an Irish pub is perfect, because Keegan is definitely my enemy.

I order a couple of pints for our guests.

"This here is Cole," Keegan says.

"Hi, Cole. I'm Maeve. This is Saoirse and Ciara."

"So where is the black fellow you ran off with, Maeve? I am surprised you can walk after spending time with him. You know what they say about those blokes," Keegan jokes.

I smile at his attempt at humor. "He is back in the States. I'm sure you would refer to anyone of any nationality in that way, considering what you are walking around with between your legs," I say and hold up my pinky finger. "And his name is Miles. Did Gemma realize what a fecking useless piece of shite you are and leave your ass yet?" I ask.

I can see that he isn't quite sure what to make of me. Could the drink be making me bolder? I see his wheels spinning in wonder.

"Funny. To answer your question, we are still married and expecting our first child," he says.

Oh goodness, this is proof if there ever was that any pair of fools can make a child. "Well, I'd congratulate you but I should be out warning the government that you are procreating."

His friend and mine are laughing at our banter.

"Seeing how you tried to off yourself because I broke up with you, seems like you would love to be in Gemma's spot right now."

I don't bat a lash. He doesn't realize that I really feel nothing toward him. "Ha! I love that you believe it had anything to do with you and nothing at all to do with what I dealt with for a year. Then I realized that being there really did save me from you! I heard my da kicked your ass over it though, and your da's at the same time!" I can't contain my giggles. I'm tired of this shite. "Cole, would you take my girls up to the bar? Order whatever you'd like, it's on me. I need to have a more intimate chat with my dear friend Keegan." I make a face on the word *friend*.

When they get up I move to the same side of the bench as Keegan. I know that I am giving up the barrier but I need him to know once and for all that I am not afraid of him. Nor do I care what he does, one way or the other.

"That was fun," I say.

"Tons," he says.

"Listen, Keegan, it is obvious that we are going to cross paths, a lot. I want you to know that I don't love you, I don't miss you, I don't think about you, and most important I don't hate you. It is what it is. It didn't work out between us and we are both ecstatic about that fact, are we not? We don't have to be friends, we don't have to be anything, or we can continue to slam each other at every opportunity. Your very existence offers a wealth of digs," I say and smile.

His turn.

"Are you sure you are over me?" He has the audacity to lean in like he is going to kiss me. My hand grabs his face without hesitation and I slam his head against the back support of the bench we are sitting on. His shock is real and my grip is not tender.

"Don't touch me."

His hands go up in defeat. "Okay."

"So, it was nice chatting with you. My girls and I are going to continue with our date." I get up and go back to my side of the bench. Another thing I learned: always face the door, another way to have more control over your environment.

Keegan has been dismissed and leaves without another word. My girls come back and bring another pint for me with them. We are going to have to grab a cab if we keep this up.

"That was fecking amazing, Maeve. Who are you?" Saoirse asks me.

"I'm me."

We continue to enjoy ourselves. Every once in a while I lock eyes with Keegan and all I can see is respect in his eyes. In the way he nods in my direction or holds his pint toward me.

I have conquered my demons. I whisper a silent prayer to god, thanking him for the strength.

I HAVE BEEN HOME for a few weeks now and have settled into my life. My boredom is real though. I have enjoyed reacquainting myself with the twins and my folks. I bump into Gemma and Keegan occasionally, and they look happy. As I promised myself, I have continued my Krav Maga training and even added some parkour classes. I tumbled as a kid and teen so it comes easy to me. The rush and agility is what draws me to both forms.

During the end of my first month home I realize what is missing in my life. Miles. I'm better now. I have proved to myself that I don't need anyone. The relationships in my life are the ones I want. Sure, I think of The Chamber once in a while, but knowing what I know now about who I am, the nightmares are gone. I'm not afraid of the things that go bump in the night. I miss so much about him. How funny he is, how much we have in common, and the look of genuine love for me that was always in his eyes.

I don't hesitate. I dial his area code and number. The phone rings a few times before he picks up.

"I was waiting for your call," his tender voice says into the receiver. It speaks volumes.

He *was* waiting for me.

EPILOGUE
MAEVE

*I*t has been two years since I picked up the phone and called Miles. We are engaged to be married and are closer than ever. I don't live in Ireland anymore. In fact, we don't really live anywhere. We live everywhere. Wherever we want. We go back and visit my folks and his father whenever we get the chance.

Right now we are in Seattle, Washington. I continue my training that is now part of my life—both of our lives. Miles is no longer guarding important people, though we are planning on putting down roots in the near future to set up our training center, so that we can teach people how to protect themselves. But that is the future. Right now we are enjoying the present which is a gift.

We don't go a day without telling each other what a gift our love is. We frequently show each other this very thing when we are making love. Miles has taken to enjoying my kinkiness and has one-upped me on several occasions.

If we have children one day we will teach them to love themselves and the skin they are in. We will teach them to protect themselves, and we will send them into the world happy and confident.

I have survived being kidnapped as a young girl, I survived The Chamber, and I have fallen in love with Maeve O'Malley.

The End

Read Eclipsed Sunshine, the next book in the Seven Chamber series.

ECLIPSED SUNSHINE SAMPLE

Chapter One
Whitney

"Are you sure it's not too much?" I ask about my new dress, *and* the makeup, *and* the fancy hair. To be honest, I feel like a doll being dressed up, and if I'm being *really* honest, this whole charade reminds of the place I don't want to speak about.

All this fuss over me, ensuring that not a hair is out of place, so that I'm the perfect play toy. I don't want to go back there in my body or mind, but too many little things remind me of the worst year of my entire life. Nothing matters though, I've been home for three weeks and most nights I wake up in a cold sweat from a dream so real that it takes an eternity before I realize I am home—I am free.

It could be something as simple as a smell that drifts through the air that brings me back to that awful room with the obnoxiously cheery yellow décor, the oversized bed fit for a queen, and the location of my worst imaginings. And somehow being home, standing here with my two best gals as they pretty me up for dinner with Thomas feels no different. In fact, it's much worse. I feel like a fraud for trying to forget what happened to me—that the last year was something I made up. My friend's think tonight is the night that Thomas is going to propose to me, just like they were so sure he was going to before I was taken. But, why would someone like me think that I deserve a happy ending, when I'm so obviously cursed?

Who am I kidding? I stare into the mirror at my reflection. Gone is the fresh-faced girl with the light brown complexion that looked at the world with hope and optimism. I fear I will never be her again.

"This is a bad idea." I pull the earrings off, grab a tissue and start wiping off the lipstick. Nothing about any of this feels right to me.

I shouldn't be doing anything but crawling into my bed. I'm always so tired. My gals don't get it, and I don't expect them to. Unless they've been where I've been, they can't.

In The Chamber my life was not my own. My body belonged to someone else. An entire year can't be erased with pretty dresses and fancy dinners. Makeup can't cover up the truth. My friends don't have horrid images burned into their memories. Their faith in humanity isn't shattered.

When they look at me I know they see a young woman who has a full life ahead of her, who should be ready to face it with a grateful smile. They can't possibly understand that I'm not that young woman anymore. She isn't inside of me. I don't feel her in my rigid smile. My heart that used to beat with excitement and joy, now only beats to sustain my life—I can't even manage to conjure up enough hope, not even for tonight. I long for butterflies in the pit of my stomach and daydreams about the future.

Chalice and Amaris had the best intentions for tonight, but if they knew what I suffered, they would know that everything about tonight reminds me of that place, my lost year.

Spending hours getting dolled up for a man is the last thing I want to do. But, one look at my friends and I can see it in their eyes— hope. They stand and watch me with hope that I'm okay, hope that things can return to normal for me and for them. They don't want me to be stuck, and I get it, neither does my mom, *or* my dad, *or* my sisters, *or* Thomas. But they aren't giving me time.

"Stop. What are you doing?" Amaris says, her warm island accent soothing, even in frustration, as she runs at me to grab the tissue from my hand. "I put a lot of work into making you look like heaven and you're wiping it all to hell."

I flop onto the edge of my bed. I can't tell them I don't want to go out. When Thomas set tonight up, I *was* excited. The idea that he has welcomed me back into his arms knowing everything I've been through is an answered prayer. And when my gals and I went dress shopping yesterday I was floating on a puffy cloud. Grateful that after everything I'd suffered I can come home and have all of this, this, normal. The icing on the cake is a date with the man whose love helped me survive my year in captivity. Maybe, I've been lying to myself, and I do deserve a happy ending.

Last night, I stared at my little green dress and imagined sitting across from Thomas and his amazing smile. I envisioned him proposing and of course, me saying yes. Thoughts of how tonight would go kept me up all night, and let's be honest, it was much better than the thoughts that normally plague me.

"I can't do this. I need to call and cancel. I'm really tired."

"Don't be foolish. You have to move on with your life, sweets. Thomas waited a whole year for you. How long do you think he will continue to wait?" Chalice asks.

I shrug my shoulders. I have no idea how long. I know if I loved someone I wouldn't implement a time limit, and I would want them at their best. I certainly wouldn't rush them after something so traumatic, but that's me. Maybe three weeks is long enough. I mean, I don't want to lose him. What Chalice is saying is harsh but true, and I'm smart enough to know that everyone will scatter if I continue to walk around with a dark cloud over my head. What else can I do? Three weeks is all they've given me.

Ignoring all the contrary feelings coursing through me, I glance around and note that this is my bedroom, not the yellow room that haunts me. In fact, there isn't a stitch of yellow in sight. My room is so different than *that* place. Thankfully.

Missing are the elaborate and ornate furnishings, the sex toys, a bed big enough for four. Gone is the groomer who tended to all my needs. In its place my best gal friends who love me and everything that is, or was, simply me.

"You're right. I have to try." I hand Amaris the tube of lipstick and she begins reapplying. While she goes to work, I think about my Thomas. We have been spending a lot of time together in the weeks that I've been home. He is everything that I remembered him to be—kind, patient, and loving. Having him to come home to lessens some of the pain from the last year. I can do this for him and for us. And if I'm lucky, tonight will be the night I dreamed it would be, the night that was stolen from me a year ago.

I stand up, walk over to the mirror and gaze at myself. It takes everything for me to not feel like I'm preparing for an entirely different night. "Thomas said dress to impress," I say in a soft voice.

"And you, my dear, are dazzling," Amaris says.

Okay, Whitney, you can do this. You are not locked away in a gothic castle. You are home in your beloved Barbados. The sun is always shining, and you are free, I say to myself as I stare at my reflection.

Amaris could work in The Chamber, she's that good. I shake my head to douse the errant thought.

My makeup is natural, just like I like it. My green dress shouts spring glamour. The hem rests about a foot above my knee and the dress clings to my curves. I feel naked. Since I've been home, I have avoided anything that makes me sexy. Baggy and loose has been my modus operandi. Standing here in this dress, I feel almost Chamber ready, and I hate myself for it. My heart is hammering in my chest and my stomach is queasy.

"What's wrong?" Chalice asks.

I don't answer her. The lump in my throat makes it hard for me to speak. When the tears spring forth from my eyes, I crawl onto my bed. My gals share the silence with me and climb onto the bed. "I don't think I can leave the house dressed like this."

"You look beautiful," Chalice says with a question in her voice.

"That's just it. I don't want to look that way," I admit.

My friends don't say anything, but I know them well and they want to.

"I know it sounds insane. But the man who took me said he loved to collect beautiful play things. Maybe if I didn't wear sexy things he would have never noticed me."

They squeeze me tighter. "How can that be true? I'm much sexier than you, sweets, and he didn't take me," Chalice teases, and it's just what I need because I burst into laughter wilted with tears.

"Seriously, though. If you change every part of who you are because of that evil monster, then you're letting him win. He already took so much from you. You can't let him have it all," Amaris says.

I nod; she's right. That's one of the things my therapist has been telling me in both my group and private sessions, and it feels right to hear it. Sometimes I feel like I'm on the path to getting back to the old me, and I want it, I need it. But then other times, when I'm not in the company of my therapist or fellow trauma survivors, it's an entirely different scenario. When my friends and family are with me, I feel so different, not like myself at all, and what's worse is they all look at me differently too. I don't think they do it on purpose; I don't think they can help themselves. Around them, I'm bare. I don't feel empowered. I don't feel strong, and I'm afraid all the time.

What if he takes me again? What if someone else does the same thing? How can I be me again? The old me? That girl is so far gone I wouldn't know her if she was standing right in front of me.

"I'll try."

The three of us sit up in my bed and share a group hug.

"I love you guys."

"We love you, too."

Amaris wipes my tears. "We're here for you, and we'll help you through this, okay?"

I nod my head and smile. But her words make the tears fall harder. I know I'm too emotional for all of this, but Thomas is so worth me trying.

"You'll be safe tonight. Thomas is tough. If there are any bad guys out there, he won't let them near you, sweets," Chalice says.

My friends are right about Thomas; he loves me and I know he can keep me safe. He has been taking things slow with me, not to the point of treating me like glass, but close. I have been as honest and transparent about what I suffered as I can.

As much as I want to forget, Thomas won't let me; he says I need to speak about it so that I can heal. As resistant as I am, my therapist says he's right and if he is someone that I can trust and open up to, it will only help me in my healing process.

Recently, Thomas confided in me about his own struggles. I think it's his way of showing his vulnerability to me. Thomas is a very proud and shrewd business man, so him trusting me with the knowledge of his recent financial woes and unemployment had to be very hard on him. He has never made our time together about him, but his honesty has made confiding in him easier—a little. He is attentive to me and my needs and promises me that we will both be okay. But I can't help but feel responsible for what he has lost. He has never come out and said that it was my fault that he lost so much, but in some way, I have to believe if I hadn't been kidnapped he'd probably be as successful as he was before I left. I can only imagine how hard it was for him while I was missing.

I almost told him about the money twice. Knowing about the four million dollars I received from Mason wouldn't just lift his mood, he could actually bounce back and return to the amazing business career he had before.

But I haven't told him; I haven't told anyone.

Even when I think I might be able to, I can't fix my mouth to say the words. Knowing how much I could help the people that I love makes me feel even more guilty for keeping this to myself. But to speak it makes what happened to me more than real.

The money makes me feel dirty.

When I do get the courage to tell him, I hope he is happy and doesn't look at me differently. This is the man I hope to spend the rest of my life with, and I plan to do everything in my power to help him—I just need to tell him when I'm ready and that isn't right now.

"Come with me," Amaris says and pulls me to stand. She sets me in the chair in front of my mirror.

She goes to work fixing my makeup. "You can do this. You deserve to look beautiful for your fiancé," Amaris says.

"He isn't my fiancé, Amaris."

"He will be after tonight, sweets," Chalice says and mists me with body spray.

I roll my eyes at them both. "I wouldn't be so sure," I say under my breath.

The doorbell rings just as Amaris finishes retouching my makeup. My stomach hits the floor.

Daddy knocks on the door and pokes his head in. "Baby, Thomas is here. You ready?"

I slip on my matching heels and follow my dad out of my bedroom door and down the hall, my girls on my heels.

"Baby, you look beautiful," Daddy says.

"Thanks, Daddy. I wish Mom was here."

He shakes his head. "She does, too. She hated leaving when you just got home. But she called today and said your grandmother is doing much better, so she and your sisters will be home before you know it," he promises and gives me a kiss on my forehead.

Thomas stands up from the sofa to greet me. He is stunning. His dark brown skin looks divine in his ocean blue suit that is tailor-made for him. "Wow, Whitney. You take my breath away," he says and takes the short steps to me. He acknowledges my gals and reaches his hand out for me. I take it. *Can he feel how moist my palms are?* If he does, he's too much of a gentleman to react to it.

"Thomas, take care of my baby," Daddy says.

"Yes, sir, I will."

Chapter Two
The Chamber, Week One

"Are you ready for tonight?" I ask Violet.

She shakes her head. "I don't think it's possible. Are you?"

I let out a long sigh and take a seat next to her on her bed. The way she has her red hair tied in a high ponytail, revealing fresh freckled skin make her appear much too young to be in a place like this. Not that my twenty years qualifies me. No person should be subjected to this horror.

Violet and I are roommates in this horrible place. It's only been a week since we were brought here. A lot has happened, but tonight is the big night. Our first night with the men in our individual rooms. My stomach churns thinking about it.

"I'm scared to death. Literally shaking." I hold my hand up and show her the tremor that has been with me since I was taken. "I don't think I can do this."

She wraps her arms around me and I copy the action. We sit in silence holding one another, comforting each other in our time of need, we both sob.

"Sunshine." A voice I am already too familiar with calls from the door.

I look up and find Layne, my groomer, standing there. I squeeze Violet. "Are we sure it's too late to try to break out?" I whisper into her ear.

"Where would we go?" she asks.

"At least we're not alone. I'll say a prayer for you," I say.

"Me too," she says.

"Iris should be along any minute for you, Violet," Layne says. If we were anywhere else her smile would be comforting. She is a beautiful woman, with long light brown hair, a lithe body, and bright green eyes. But she works here; she is one of them. According to Mason, our groomers are supposed to be our right-hand person in this place. The way I see it, if you work here, you can't be trusted.

I follow Layne through the zigzagging halls. When we arrive at the spa Flame, Sky, and Raven are already there. We offer each other smiles that were meant to comfort, but instead relay our fears. Within a few minutes the room fills with all seven of us, and our groomers. We sit in salon chairs, while the groomers, poke and prod, smooth and tweeze. Lane reclines my chair and instructs me to flip over onto my stomach. She gives me the most amazing massage I have ever had.

I feel a hand graze my skin. I raise my hand in search of the touch and grasp the hand of the person next to me—Sky.

Tears spill from my eyes and hit the floor below me. I can't believe this is my life.

"Ladies. Ladies. It's time!" Mason's deep voice breaks through the silence.

Layne steps away from me, and I sit up on the edge of my seat. I lock eyes with Mason, for a brief second, before his gaze slides down to admire each of us. A smile on his face—pride. A cold shiver shoots through my body.

"We have no time to waste. The lucky winners are already here waiting. Make me proud," he says, then turns on his heel and walks out."

None of us says a word, but the energy is palpable—fear.

Layne sits next to me. "We have to go. I still need to get you dressed."

Like a doll that isn't capable of dressing itself, I follow her back through the maze and into my chamber—yellow everywhere, so much yellow. On the bed, on the walls. Not the furniture, that's dark wood. I follow Layne to my chamber bathroom. She makes fast work of sweeping my hair into a messy updo, and I step into a sleek yellow gown that is completely sheer, held together by two ties that are like nooses against my skin.

"Beautiful," Layne says.

"Montreal is at the bottom of the stairs, should you need anything. Good luck."

Layne slips away, leaving me alone. Before I have a chance to panic, a man is standing in the doorway—my first visitor for the night.

"Sunshine, you are dazzling," he says. The man stalks forward. He is tall, well over six feet with deep olive-skin, and a muscular build. I stay put as he crosses the room to me. While I do my best to control my breathing—even still my head swirls and gets light. Passing out would be the best and worst thing for me to do right now.

I've had sex before. I have a boyfriend, had a boyfriend. But never like this, against my will. Prettied up like a doll for this man, and the many others waiting their turn.

"Call me, Connell."

He is so close to me. His hand grazes my arm, leaving cold in its wake. "I've put my name in the hat for two years to get a coveted spot in Mason's fuck-fest. I plan to make every second memorable, starting with you. His lips are on mine, at first gentle, almost sweet. I kiss him back, afraid of what would happen if I chose instead to stand mannequin still.

"Yes, Sunshine." He breathes into my mouth as he undoes the bottom tie.

My breath catches in my throat. Tremors rattle through me. My dress gathers into a puddle on the floor between us. My mind goes to my family, Thomas. I will never survive this, but I have to. He steps back and stares at me. He motions for me to spin around and my stomach rolls with nausea when he whistles his appreciation.

"Fucking splendid," he says and cups one of my breasts in his hand and begins licking and slurping my nipple. "Are you wet for me?" he asks and plunges an unknown number of fingers deep inside me. "Fuck yeah you are."

Tears begin pooling in my eyes, and I tip my head back trying to coax them back to where they came from—epic fail. Instead they roll down the sides of my face. I swipe them quick and pretend to have brought my arms up to play in his hair.

"You like that?" he asks.

"Yes." I lie. My heart is pounding through my chest.

I gasp when he picks me up. He holds onto my ass and tosses me onto the bed. He stares down at me, his chest rising and falling as he stares down at me. More tears invade, and I don't attempt to wipe them.

"Don't be afraid, love. Sex is a beautiful thing. Time has made it into something more intimate and personal." He watches me as he unbuttons his shirt, slow and deliberate, never taking his eyes off me.

I fight the sobs that want to break through.

"Animals in nature don't need to court each other. A dog can walk up to another dog on the street, fuck it senseless and go about its day. Humans assigned labels to sex. When it is primal and organic, it's like an addictive drug."

His shirt falls to the floor. He is as strong as he looked clothed. A chest and abdomen that is rippled with muscles, not bulky, but tight and hard. Dark hair lightly covers his chest and trails down his stomach. I tear my eyes from his body when his hands go for his belt.

"I won't be gentle, but I promise to leave you wanting so much more."

When his pants hit the floor, my body shakes more. But I don't have much time to contemplate my immediate future. He falls forward in a swift motion and sinks his cock inside of me. My eyes widen to double their size with the fullness of him. He watches me, as he pulls out of me and slams back inside of me, over and over. My body takes over despite my fight for it not to do so. Traitorous moans escape me, my back arches wanting more.

"Feel it, Sunshine."

He pushes deep inside of me and stays there this time, moving his hips in circles, punishing me with his fullness. I match his motions until I come apart, my body slamming into his and pushing so hard my bones ache. I shake and shutter, and yell out.

"My turn," he says and flips me over onto my stomach, pulling me onto my knees.

He grabs onto my ass and pulls until my back is arched in the extreme. "I am going to fuck you so hard you'll dream about me." He pushes inside me, slower this time. Moaning as he does it. Then he raises my legs off the bed. While holding onto them, he picks up speed, pumping his cock inside of me with desperation, until he shouts and squeezes my skin, filling me with his essence.

I collapse onto the bed, and he falls next to me.

"What do you think? Carnal. Not scary?"

I don't say what I'm thinking, which is: yes, it would be if I met you at a club and made the decision to do this with you. "Still scary, but you made it less scary. Yes, carnal."

He runs his fingers through my hair. Unexpected.

"We are going to be spending a lot of time together. In time it won't be scary at all, I promise. Thank you for being my first."

My eyes get big. *His first?*

"Chambermaid, I mean."

He kisses me on the lips, grabs his clothes and leaves.

Chapter Three
Whitney

The restaurant is gorgeous—the kind of place you spend hours getting dressed up for—located inside of the lavish Crane Beach Hotel that sits near the water.

Thomas leans forward and says to the host. "Reservation for two under Thomas Ackerly." The man scans a tablet for our reservation. Thomas oozes power and confidence. No one would ever guess at him having money problems. Maybe my gals were right and he is planning a romantic proposal. Otherwise, why would a man with money problems bring his girlfriend to such an expensive restaurant. "I requested a table near the window overlooking the ocean," he continues.

"Yes, sir. I believe your table is ready."

I fidget when the host smiles and stares at me too long. Thrusting me back into my uncomfortable place. Thomas pulls me closer to him. He feels it too.

The gentleman takes us to our table and like Thomas requested, we are seated along a series of windows overlooking the water. "Beautiful," I say. I can only imagine how amazing the view will be when the sun sets. Thomas pulls my seat out for me.

Wow, he makes me feel special.

"Good evening, and welcome to L'Azure," a waitress says, her islander accent like a soothing song. The two of us look up. "Would you like to start with a drink?"

Thomas clears his throat. "Your best champagne," he says.

I watch him as he commands attention. He has always had this powerful presence, as if he is leagues more important in status than he is. I know that's one reason he brought me here, even when he and I both know this place is too expensive. He knows his worth. Which is why he has always been so successful in business, and another reason that I believe in my heart that he will land on his feet and bounce back quickly. I hope the same for myself.

When the waitress leaves, I brace myself to say what's on my mind. "Thomas, I know you want to make tonight special, but maybe you shouldn't spend so much money. I'd be fine with a lot less—" I glance around the room, "—extravagance."

Thomas slides his hand over mine. "Darling, everything is fine. I've got an amazing deal in the works that will change everything." His smile is dazzling.

This news cheers me up. I have too much in my life to feel guilty for, and Thomas' career getting back on track would take one thing off my heavily loaded plate. "That's fantastic news, Thomas. You deserve all the success."

He flashes me a dashing smile before saying, "*We* deserve it."

A man comes to our table with champagne and two glasses. He opens the bottle, fills our glasses with flair, leaving the bottle.

"Whitney, a year ago when you went missing, I went crazy. I was lost without you. I didn't care about my business or anything else, just finding you." He raises his glass. But I don't join him in the action. The lump finds my throat again and it takes everything in my body not to cry. I risk ruining such a beautiful night by turning into a slobbering baby.

"I'm sorry for what you lost," I manage to say to him.

He takes my hand and sets his glass down.

"Nothing to be sorry about. I'm resilient, and now that you're home I feel like I can do anything. This is a cause for celebration, not tears, eh." He picks up his glass again and gestures for me to pick up mine, and I do. "To the love of my life coming back to me," he says, and we both take a drink. The champagne is refreshing and the perfect amount of sweet. Delicious. My eyes catch the familiar little blue velvet box as Thomas places it on the table.

I gasp. "Thomas." I set my glass down and look at him, stunned.

He is so good-looking and confident. The kind of guy most parents dream of their daughter finding. Handsome, strong, intelligent. I count myself as lucky enough to be sitting opposite this man that still wants me.

Thomas opens the box. The ring is stunning, but simple. A white gold band with a single solitaire, surrounded by a bouquet of three rows of smaller diamonds. "It's beautiful," I say.

He snaps the box shut. "Tonight, I plan to make all of your dreams come true. But I need a favor."

My face must bare my confusion. *What favor could possibly be tied to a proposal?* "Anything," I say.

Thomas leans forward and I mimic the action. "There's a man upstairs. A client."

I don't say anything because I have no idea what he's talking about.

Thomas gets up from his chair and moves it around the table to sit next to me. "I want us to go into business together, become a team."

"I don't understand. What kind of team?"

His smile broadens. "The client is going to pay me twenty-five hundred dollars to spend a couple of hours with you."

There is no way that I'm hearing him right. This man that I love. I know that my brain twisted what he actually said into something heart-wrenching and horrific. Because if what I think he said is in fact what he said, then my world will tip on its axis.

"I couldn't have heard you right. What is this client expecting me to do with him for a couple of hours?"

"Don't you see? This is the answer to everything. We'd be in business together. I'm not asking you to do anything you haven't done before, only this time it won't be by force. It'll be empowering now because you're choosing to do this, completely consensual, and best of all, you'll be paid. We'll be paid." His smile is wide and proud.

I sit and stare at this man I just realized I can't possibly know, not really. I have no words.

After everything I've been through, this is how he sees me? Has he always seen me this way?

I can only manage to stare at him, no, through him. The sounds in the restaurant become muffled, lost in the background. The only sound I can hear is the thudding of my heart as it pulses loudly throughout my body.

He takes my hands into his. I don't give them to him freely or pull them away; it's as though part of me isn't here anymore. My body is numb, like I'm not sitting at this table in this beautiful oceanfront restaurant, next to the man who was supposed to love me but just offered me the equivalent of a knife to my chest, piercing my heart with monstrous precision.

Nothing in my year-long captivity could have prepared me for this moment. Dreaming of reuniting with Thomas gave me hope and strength in my darkest time. I believed he could save me from my nightmares. I could have never prepared myself for this reality...he is my nightmare.

Even as the tears roll down my cheeks, the excitement in his voice never wanes.

Ignoring my reaction, he continues, "I've given this a lot of thought. If you spend ten hours a week working we'd clean up, twenty-five thousand a week, a hundred thousand a month. Eventually, we'll hire more women and you can sit back and collect money. What do you think?"

I snatch my hand from his as if it were on fire. I swallow hard and stare.

He is Mason.

Is this how monsters begin? It's like all the superhero movies. Some characters get their powers and immediately do good, I guess because good is inside of them. While others turn to the dark side and want to hurt people, conquer or rule the world. Obviously, the darkness was always inside of them. And here I sit, next to the man I thought I loved, and I'm seeing him for the first time. Thomas is shrouded in darkness. But I still love him—it's not that easy to turn love off.

I wipe my face with the back of my hands. They shake as I bring them up to my face. When I look into his eyes they are alight and expectant. He is so sure of his plan. The background noises return and I glance around at the patrons of this beautiful establishment. I'd bet all the money Mason paid me that none of the other women here have boyfriends that believe they are whores. I could simply stand up and walk away. I'm sure Daddy could be here in less than twenty minutes, and the second I tell him what Thomas wants his precious youngest daughter to do he would promptly kick his ass. I stare at the rolling sea, I give attention to the wait staff bustling around, anything but the monster at my table. After eons pass, I finally turn my attention to Thomas, and try to appeal to his senses.

"What you're asking me to do is illegal."

He scoots closer to me, taking his hand and running it up and down my thigh. A motion twenty minutes ago I would have counted as romantic, but now, is making my skin crawl.

"We'll be discrete, only top tier clientele, and we don't have to do this forever, just until I get on my feet," he says.

I look down at the table. The tears come back. I couldn't stop them if I wanted to. My heart physically hurts from beating so hard and fast. My stomach is in knots. Come to think of it my head hurts too, the pain slamming against my skull. This is what I couldn't wait to come back to? Is this how everyone sees me? My family? My friends? After everything I went through, this is what I've been reduced to?

"Why are you so upset, eh?" he has the nerve to ask.

It takes everything I have not to shout, create a scene. "Are you serious? You thought I'd love this idea? Did you think I enjoyed my time being passed around from man to man? I was kidnapped, Thomas. I didn't join some sex club." I throw my hands to my face and take deep breaths before continuing. "You thought I'd come home and jump at the chance to screw the entire island?" I pause, trying to catch my breath. "I'm seeing a therapist because of what happened to me. I'm in a trauma survivors group, Thomas. I have nightmares, almost every night."

I stare at him with pleading eyes. I need him to see me differently, to love me the way I imagined he would. I beg him to be the man I came home for.

"Can you do this for me? For us?" he asks, ignoring everything I just said.

My attention switches focus from his eyes, and drifts across the table to the little blue box. I can't believe how excited I was moments ago. The box held with it the promise of love and happily ever after. Now I realize it is only the start of a dark and twisted fairytale, where nothing but heartache happens in the end. Why did I think I deserved more?

A heavy sigh escapes me. I am mentally exhausted. If the man who is supposed to love me sees me this way, maybe this is all that I am, all that I have left. A chambermaid forever. I look up at Thomas, into his hopeful eyes. "I'll do it."

Thomas' face registers surprise. "Really?" He beams. "You've made me the happiest man alive. I can't wait to marry you." He kisses me on the lips. It isn't sweet or gentle. He slides me a room key, wasting no time.

Wow, I don't even get dinner.

"He's waiting for you upstairs. Baby, thank you. This is the start of something big."

I'm sick to my stomach. I stand on shaky legs, reach for my champagne glass and down it, pour another and down it. I take the room key in my hand and start to walk away.

Thomas grabs my hand. "Baby, I love you."

I don't respond. The champagne is hitting me and I need it right now. I walk away. When I'm almost out of the restaurant, I glance back at Thomas to watch as he orders from the menu. My stomach heaves a couple of times, and it's all that I can do to make it to the ladies' room to deposit what little I have in my stomach. I stand in front of the mirror, rinse my mouth out and stare at my reflection. My hazel eyes look like Christmas, sharing the space with the red that has clouded them from crying.

I can't believe I held hope for coming home to him. How could I have been so stupid to think he was worth coming home to? He doesn't love me. He never did. If I give him this we will never be together, I know that. And even if we made it through this nightmare, will I even want him? I don't know if I want him now.

But what if he's the best that I deserve? What if no one else wants me but him? I'm all used up, what do I expect? How do you tell someone that you spent a year locked away, being passed around by thirty-five different men? No regular, normal guy is going to want me after all the hell I went through.

"Maybe crazy deserves crazy," I say to my reflection. At least I wouldn't be alone. I splash water on my face taking care not to wet my hair. I grab the room key from the counter and head up to the sixth floor.

Continue reading Eclipsed Sunshine

AFTERWORD

Did you love Poisoned Ivy? Be sure to review it on Amazon and let other romance readers know what you thought!

💋 Dionne

MAILING LIST

Did you enjoy Broken Sky be sure to join my mailing list and get the inside scoop on new releases, and have access to unreleased short stories about the characters you love!

.

D.W. MARSHALL'S DARK HEARTS

Want to talk with other romance lovers? Join my Facebook Group, D.W. Marshall's Dark Hearts.

ALSO BY D.W. MARSHALL

Read More of The Seven Chambers Series

The Seven Chambers Series

Stolen Flame

Weeping Violet

Shattered Sapphire

Poisoned Ivy

Eclipsed Sunshine

Cruel Obsessions Series

Twisted Soul

Coming Soon Twisted Heart

The Men of the Seven Chambers Series

Dominic

The Escorts Series

ACKNOWLEDGMENTS

It is an amazing experience to create a fictional world. There are days when I have felt overwhelmed on this journey, and a couple of times when I wanted to quit. The reason I can't quit is because writing is a part of me, it is in my soul. The pen has saved my life on many occasions growing up, giving me a safe place to express my fears, my dreams, and even pain. What I'm thankful for is the support of so many people on my journey.

Of course, my husband, mom, my nieces and nephews, my friends, my son's, and my readers are all crucial in keeping me happy and focused. My Las Vegas chapter of RWA for sharing the highs and lows of this indie writing world. Specifically, I would like to thank Heidi, thank you for designing another beautiful cover. Danylle Salinas and Danielle Acee, for making sure my I's are dotted and my T's are crossed. Dang, I would not make it through the maze that is indie publishing without you, thank you for putting your time and faith in me.

ABOUT THE AUTHOR

D.W. Marshall is a graduate of Tuskegee University. She is a native of California, but grew up in Las Vegas. If you opened her purse you'd find too many pens for one person, lip balm, and the dreaded receipts that never seem to go away.

D.W. loves to read dark *and* sweet romance, fantasy, YA, thrillers, and lives in Las Vegas with her husband, two sons, niece, and her one-eyed Bichon, named Sadie.

www.dwmarshallbooks.com